A PYRRHIC VICTORY

Also by
Frank F. Fiore

The Ijin Trilogy
In the Hands of the Gods
A Pyrrhic Victory
A Quest for Justice

The Chronicles of Jeremy Nash
A Taste of the Apocalypse
Seed
Black Sun

Cyberkill
The Oracle
Murran

I j i n

Volume 2

A PYRRHIC VICTORY

a novel

FRANK F. FIORE

WordCrafts Press

A Pyrrhic Victory
Copyright © 2019
Frank F. Fiore

ISBN: 978-1-962218-50-4

Cover concept and design by Mike Parker.
Cover photo: Imperial Japanese Army Soldier, public domain

Originally published in a single volume under the title of *Ijin: A Quest for Justice*.

Published by WordCrafts Press
Cody, Wyoming 82414
www.wordcrafts.net

To my Dad
A member of the Greatest Generation.

–RIDERS ON THE STORM–

1942 to 1944

War Fever

On the morning of December 9th, Connor came in for breakfast and immediately noticed Miyoko, Suki, and Kenji gathered around the radio, their faces all drawn with despair. He also felt the absence of the usual morning music, replaced instead with an announcer speaking rapidly and with great urgency much too fast for Connor to understand. The radio then cut to playing *The Warship March*.

He looked at Miyoko, and her face held a look of disbelief. "Miyoko," Connor said. "*Nan desu-ka?* What's going on?"

"Senso da," she replied soulfully. "We are at war with America."

As the news first swept through the country, there was an air of stifling incomprehension amongst the people. Did Japan really go to war? Except for the intermittent blackout drills every day, life seemed ordinary. The only real change was the immediate issuance of rationing. Ration books were issued to every household, but the actual distribution of food would be through the various Neighborhood Associations.

But soon, war fever quickly spread like an unchecked brush fire. Pro-war demonstrations and military parades could be seen in almost every major city. Men, women, and even school children marched to martial music, enthusiastically waving little paper Japanese flags.

Several days after the attack on Pearl Harbor, there were a series of huge rallies in Tokyo, including the *Crush America and Britain* rally, the *National Rally on the Propagation of the War Rescript*, and the *Axis Pact Certain Victory Promotion* military rally. Some of the rallies were linked to spiritual mobilization and took place in Shinto shrines. Other victory rallies would follow, maintaining the populace at a high military fervor.

But support for the war was not absolute. Not *all* rallies were in support of the war.

The Protest

"Traitors!" cried Goro. His voice echoed in the cavernous Yakuza warehouse. He had rushed into the meeting room to join Connor, Kodo, Jiro, and other Yakuza. He paced the room, waving a red leaflet that depicted a *ukiyo*-style picture of a woman with a tiger-like animal at her throat and was captioned *Deceived by Military Authorities*.

"Thousands of these have been dropped from rooftops in Tokyo," Goro roared. "They're announcing an anti-war rally at the Omura Masuijiro statue in the Yasukuni Shrine." His voice seethed with indignation. "How dare these cowards dishonor the name of Omura Masuijiro, the father of our modern military."

"They must pay for this," Kodo agreed.

"And they will," Goro replied. "We have been ordered to break up that demonstration. We leave tomorrow morning for Tokyo."

Connor nodded his head in agreement along with his fellow Yakuza. Even though he was an American and a war with his maternal country had commenced, he felt this opportunity could prove his loyalty to his adopted country. At the same time, being part of the Yakuza made him feel safe. Now that war had broken out, he had no idea how an American on the streets of Japan would be treated. He knew he needed protection.

The next day, Kodo, Connor, and twenty other Yakuza, led by Goro, strode confidently from the Tokyo Central train station to the Yasukuni Shrine armed with clubs and knives.

Connor felt strange carrying a club, but he went along with the group without question.

As they approached the shrine, the Yakuza were immediately incensed by seeing hundreds of demonstrators around the Omura Masuijiro statue. The demonstrators were holding large banners decrying the war and shouting antiwar slogans. Many of them were wearing Communist Party armbands.

Goro wasted no time in taking action. "Attack!" he ordered. "Show them what *real* patriots are."

The Yakuza did as instructed, diving into the crowd of demonstrators, violently and ruthlessly clubbing at them as they tore through the mob.

Connor found himself standing back and watching the brutal scene unfold before him. He flinched when Goro ran up behind an unsuspecting young woman and smashed his club alongside her head. The young woman collapsed in a heap to the ground, blood oozing from her skull.

Connor watched in stunned silence as Kodo hurled herself into the melee, slashing a young man across his chest who held a Communist placard above his head. He dropped his sign and fell to his knees, reaching at the gaping wound at his torso.

The other Yakuza were equally brutal, clubbing and hitting demonstrators, and herding them away from the statue.

Connor was shaken at the unfettered brutality exhibited by the Yakuza, and especially that of Kodo whose face displayed a rage of immeasurable proportions. Connor felt she must have reached down into the brutality of her own life in order to unleash such anger.

Suddenly, from behind him, Connor heard the wail of sirens. He turned to see truckloads of police arriving at the scene. A torrent of Tokkō secret police surged out from the trucks and rushed into the middle of the melee.

The Tokkō surrounded the conflict and fired rounds of tear gas indiscriminately into the crowd. The herd of people, demonstrators and Yakuza alike, rushed away from the oncoming police clad in riot gear. It suddenly became an *everyone for themselves* mentality as the Tokkō matched the brutality of the Yakuza, beating anyone within reach with batons. People ran in every direction in blind panic, and some older men and women were stampeded under foot in the growing chaos.

Connor felt he was witnessing an unbridled version of hell.

He spotted Kodo in the crowd, only to see a canister explode at her feet sending waves of tear gas into her face. She gagged violently, and a stream of uncontrollable tears flowed from her eyes obscuring her vision. She stumbled through the crowd blindly and ended up face-to-face with a Tokkō.

The Tokkō officer grabbed the young girl by the neck and punched Kodo square in the face. She fell to the ground, writhing in pain, her face now covered in blood and tears.

But that was not the end of it.

The Tokkō pulled his pistol and, without hesitation, shot her point-blank.

Kodo howled in pain, clutching at her left leg above the knee, as she thrashed on the ground. "Goro!" she yelled, waving a bloodied hand towards him. "Help me!"

But Goro just stared at her before retreating amongst the crowd.

Connor dashed toward Goro and snatched him by the arm. "We've got to help her!" he cried.

Goro yanked his arm free. "Sacrifices must be made," and he ran from the chaos.

Connor was about twenty yards from Kodo when he saw the Tokkō take aim again at her helpless form. Just as he was about to shoot, a middle-aged man collided with the officer sending the Tokkō reeling. This distraction allowed Connor the time to reach Kodo and drag her behind some protective bushes.

Safe for the moment, Kodo stared up at Connor. "Domo. Domo arigato," she said softly and placed a gentle kiss on his lips.

"We have to get you to a hospital."

"There's one not far from the shrine," she replied weakly.

Connor eased Kodo to her feet and helped her stand by his side. They looked back at the tragedy that started out as a peaceful demonstration, then turned and made their way down the street.

Taka's Glory

"We are at war with America!" shouted Taka Onado as he ran through his sleeping quarters. Yoshi and Kuro Kobayashi, his bunkmates, both shot up with a start in their hammocks.

"War?!" Kuro exclaimed.

"With America?!" Yoshi followed.

Taka waved a small sheet of paper at his two *Sen'yu*—war comrades. "Our naval air forces attacked Pearl Harbor in Hawaii yesterday, sinking many American warships. It was a glorious victory!"

Kuro clapped in approval but Yoshi responded in a much more reserved manner. He immediately thought of his home and what the war would mean to his family. His thoughts also went to his brother, Connor. An American, perhaps deemed an enemy, living in Japan.

"What's the matter, Yoshi?" Taka asked. "Aren't you proud of our navy?"

Yoshi gave a slight nod.

Taka was about to question Yoshi's lack of enthusiasm when Kuro interrupted. "Your brother is a fighter pilot. Do you think he was in on the attack?"

"Perhaps. He was assigned to an aircraft carrier just before I left."

Taka read over the war notice in his hand and stated bluntly, "We, too, will be bathed in glory soon. Just like your brother."

Yoshi nodded again, but said nothing.

✶ ✶ ✶

Taka's *soon* came quicker than anyone expected.

Yoshi's transport had been steaming south from Japan for the better part of December 1941. Then, one early morning, Sgt. Gunso, their platoon leader, entered the unit's sleeping quarters on the troop transport.

Gunso was quite large for a Japanese; a big, burly man, and as intimidating as any sergeant could ever be. Rumor around the platoon was that he came from a family of sumo wrestlers, but that he himself couldn't qualify for the sport. He was considered the *runt* of the litter, but no man in the platoon would ever dare say that directly to his face.

"Out of your bunks and fall into formation," he instructed in a gruff voice. "We have received our orders."

There was a din of silence and a discernible holding of breath in the sleeping bay.

"As you already know, we are at war with America. The first elements of our invasion fleet arrived at their objective several days ago and have invaded. You will soon join them." He paused for the proper effect. "Our objective is the Philippine Islands."

Yoshi and Kuro gasped. Such an objective! Not just an island that they had speculated on, but an *entire country*.

Gunso continued with their orders. "We assault the beaches in a few days. Prepare yourselves and be at the ready. That is all." With that said, he turned and marched out of the bay.

"We have already landed troops!" cried Taka.

"And I guess we'll be bathing in Taka's glory soon," Kuro added.

First Taste of Battle

Those few days came soon enough.

As the sun rose over the horizon, the three Sen'yu stood at the railing of their troop transport waiting to board a landing craft. None of them spoke. Instead, each mulled over their own private thoughts—excitement, pride, and fear of the unknown. They clutched their Type 38 field rifles and wore mushroom-shaped tetsu-bo battle helmets that displayed the five-pointed star of the Imperial Japanese Army.

Yoshi fingered his hooked guard bayonet at his side, and hoped he would not be forced to use the resourceful weapon against the enemy. Face to face combat could be brutal. Though due to his training, he knew he could easily lock the blade of an adversary with the hook guard by a twist of his wrist, thereby disarming his opponent.

Just hours before, the men were informed that Manila, the capital of the Philippines, had fallen, and that Yoshi's unit would join others on the final push to free Luzon from U.S. forces.

Taka, as always, was eager to engage in combat. "The Americans are melting before us. Like we were told, their decadent democracy has raised only cowards."

Perhaps, thought Yoshi. But he himself had seen much courage in his adopted American brother. This fight might not be as easy as Taka predicted.

Soon, they boarded the landing craft and were approaching the beach. The ocean swells undulated under their transport as Yoshi's anxiety, combined with the erratic up and down motion of the landing craft, started to make him feel seasick. He held down his bile through sheer determination.

He would soon need that determination in the face of combat.

Suddenly, high above him, the sound of plane engines roared through the sky.

"Look," Kuro exclaimed. "Our planes."

"No," Sgt. Gunso corrected as he looked through his binoculars at the large aircraft approaching them. "American planes. B-17 bombers."

The entire troop inside the landing craft watched as a dozen bombers approached the invasion fleet. When they were directly above it, the B-17s dropped a blanket of bombs over the ships. Most missed, raising plumes of white water high in the sky as the bombs exploded.

But a few of the bombs hit their targets, damaging two transports and a light cruiser.

"Where are our planes?" Taka shouted.

"There!" Gunso responded as six Zeros appeared overheard and chased after the B-17s. The Zeros buzzed around the large bombers like small insects, laying tracer fire into their metal shells. Two of the B-17s burst into smoke and flames, and spun into the ocean.

The aerial show was interrupted by the landing craft suddenly colliding with the beachhead. Yoshi and the others were tossed forward by the blunt impact. "Everyone out," shouted Gunso, and the landing craft dumped the troops into knee-deep water.

Yoshi and the other soldiers ran through the low surf, hit the soft beach, and took cover along a line of trees and scrub bush just beyond the sand.

Lying prone on the wet sand beside Taka and Kuro, Yoshi could hear the sound of gunfire rattle down the beach, followed by several distant explosions.

"Somebody found some action," Taka declared. "Let's move down the beach and join them."

At that moment Gunso appeared behind them. "Get up and move inland," he growled.

The three boys stood up and followed Gunso into the sparse forest that soon turned into a thicket. The sergeant led them through some thick underbrush and out onto a dirt road.

"Look out," yelled Kuro just as a Japanese tank on their left rumbled past them.

"Fall in behind our tank," Gunso ordered.

The three Sen'yu and a squad of others dutifully followed the Type 95 light tank down the road through what was now a jungle which was thick with trees and stood eerily quiet as the column of troops, tanks, and motorized vehicles advanced down the road. Several minutes later, the road led through a cane forest, and it reminded Yoshi of the beautiful cane woodland near Tokyo that his father would take the family to on occasion.

Yoshi was about to share his reflections with Kuro when a sound like air escaping out of a balloon interrupted the silence.

"Down," screamed Gunso as he shoved Yoshi and Kuro into the dirt.

Several mortar rounds immediately detonated so close to them that the ground shook under Yoshi's face, his bones vibrated, and the smell of cordite stung at his nose. Another exploded in front of him, then another. This time, Yoshi experienced even worse trauma—it felt as if he was clubbed upside the head with a brick. He reached up and felt two indentations in his helmet, then immediately thrust three fingers under the steel shell, expecting to feel blood, but felt nothing instead—his helmet absorbed the blast.

"Into the trench," bellowed an order from somewhere, and every soldier complied, crab walking to the edge of the road.

Yoshi threw himself into the trench, followed by Kuro and Taka, who landed next to him—or more like *on* him.

More mortar rounds exploded around them, followed by the screaming of metal shrapnel that caused the sides of the trench to crumble around them.

The three of them, along with several other soldiers, scrambled out of the trench and into the protection of the cane forest, falling mortars exploding around them as they ran through dirt, blood, and body parts erupting into the sky like confetti around them.

Yoshi dropped to the ground and pressed his face deep into the muck and mire of the forest floor, then chanced a look back at the road and saw the cause of the explosion. A Japanese tank stood on its side, sliced open like a discarded sardine can. The dead tank operator hung from the wreckage, his burning flesh bubbling from the flames that engulfed him.

Yoshi wretched the contents of his stomach and forced his eyes from the carnage when a hand grabbed him on the shoulder. "Move," Gunso barked and pointed back to the road.

Yoshi joined Taka and Kuro, who like Yoshi, had their first taste of death carved on their faces.

The shelling stopped as suddenly as it started, and the column of troops, tanks, and motorized vehicles began to advance once again.

The trio was silent as they trudged forward. They had nothing to say as each replayed their first true experience of combat and gruesome death in their heads. In a few weeks they would see more much, and Yoshi would experience the true nature of the Imperial Army.

And he would never forget.

Doubt

"Private Fujiyama," Gunso said as Yoshi sat on the dirt, devouring his field rations. The platoon was embracing a spate of calm before moving forward once again. Except for the mortar attack, the last several days in their advance had been almost uneventful.

Almost.

Yoshi and his comrades saw dozens of deserted and torched vehicles and civilian houses. In addition, one large village had been entirely burned down. Nothing remained.

Eventually, all the villages they passed were reduced to charred fields, and no local inhabitants were seen.

"Yes, sir," he responded to Gunso.

"There's someone here that wants to see you." Gunso turned to an Infantry Captain, saluted, and left.

Yoshi, seeing the officer, arose to salute.

The Captain motioned for him to stay seated. "My name is Captain Soji Okada, and I promised your sister Suki that I would look you up after she told me that we were in the same unit."

Captain Okada took a seat next to Yoshi and explained how he met Suki in the military hospital in Kobe. "So? You are well I take it? And I assume you've seen some combat."

Yoshi nodded and lowered his eyes. "Hai. But it wasn't as glorious as we were led to believe." He looked back to Okada. "In fact, we are told very little about what is happening and where are we are going."

"I see. Well, except for light resistance, the enemy has melted before our advance."

Yoshi sensed the irony in Okada's voice. "You don't believe that?" Okada kept his eyes leveled on the young man but said nothing.

Yoshi filled the lull in the conversation. "I *did* hear that the roads heading south are jammed with enemy soldiers who had abandoned their arms and equipment in order to escape our infantry, armored columns, and planes."

"Hai. It's true that Manila has fallen, and that the Americans are retreating, but there are reports of many losses on our side as well." Okada sighed. "In our regiment alone, over sixty percent of the NCOs and soldiers, and nearly all the officers, have been eliminated."

Yoshi remained quite. *Was that to be his fate as well?*

Okada gazed toward the arcing sun over the southern mountains that stood populated with sprawling green trees. "That's where we are going. The Bataan Peninsula. The enemy will make its final stand there."

He returned his gaze on the young man and patted Yoshi on the shoulder. "Be courageous. Be brave. And above all, don't dishonor yourself or your family."

Yoshi gave a weak nod, but then quickly stood erect and gave Okada a respectful salute.

Fear and Anxiety

"I'm afraid," whispered Miyoko. "I'm afraid for our family. I'm afraid for our entire country."

The family, including Fujiyama, Suki, Kenji, and Connor, were listening to the latest war news on the radio accompanied by martial music. The normal program at that time was supposed to be the *Women's Hour*, but it had been replaced with the *Home at War Hour*, peppered with war propaganda.

"Not the best music to digest breakfast to," Kenji sniffed.

"We've told you before, Kenji, keep your opinions to yourself," Miyoko replied softly. "You can get in trouble. You can get us *all* in trouble." Suddenly overcome with fear of the unknown, she rushed from the room with tears in her eyes.

Fujiyama sighed and addressed his children, "These are troublesome times. Dangerous times. Please watch what you do and say to your mother." He turned his attention to Connor. "I want you to stay close to home. You are an American. No matter how Japanese you may think you are, and even though you are part of this family, that will mean nothing to the fanatics out on the streets."

Connor disagreed but nodded. He felt *protected*, and he wanted to tell that to his adopted father but knew he couldn't. If Fujiyama knew he was with the Yakuza, it would not bode well for anyone.

Fujiyama excused himself to the bedroom where he found Miyoko sitting on the bed. He sat beside her and took her hand in his.

She turned doleful eyes to her husband. "Will we win?"

"I don't know. The attack on America is more an attack on the country's will than her installations and armed forces. I'm afraid that our victories so far have instilled in us the *victory disease*. An arrogance that sees the enemy as weak and corrupt."

He squeezed her hand tighter. "But Yamamoto believes the American Navy is still a threat no matter how many victories the Army has achieved against the Americans and British." He kissed her on the cheek. "I meet with Yamamoto today. Perhaps I can come home with more positive news."

He stood to leave when Miyoko tugged on his hand. "What of Hiyakawa? What of his wife?"

"Hiyakawa has been interned by the Americans, as we have interned *their* ambassador and staff. The diplomats will be exchanged soon. I hope. As for his wife… I don't know. I'll keep trying to locate her."

"Please be careful. The fanatics are war crazy," Miyoko pleaded.

He attempted to give her a reassuring smile. "I'll be careful. You as well. Now, go about your work at the hospital."

Operation MI

Thirty minutes later, Fujiyama was in the war room of the Nagato with Yamamoto and his staff. Chief of Staff, Admiral Matome Ugaki pored over maps of the central Pacific on a large table in front of him.

"The American Navy is still a threat," Yamamoto stated. "American aircraft carriers raided our strongholds in the Gilbert and Marshall Islands during the last weeks." He stabbed the map of Hawaii with his finger. "Because of Nagumo's cautiousness and the unfortunate luck of missing the American carriers at Pearl Harbor, America still has a functioning base in Hawaii and carriers to threaten our homeland."

"And the Naval General Staff agrees with you?" Fujiyama asked.

Yamamoto shook his head. "No. We are driving the Allies back everywhere in the Pacific. The NGS believe our islands are unreachable, and even if the Americans do not surrender, they are deemed a minimal threat." He swept his hand over the large map before him. "The southern width of Japan's new empire is 6,400 miles. North to south, it is 5,300 miles. Our defensive perimeter now stretches 14,200 miles, more than half the distance around the globe."

Yamamoto tapped his pen against the table. "We hope that America will lose the resolve to fight. But if we're wrong, we need to disarm her so there is no question of surrender." He pointed at Hawaii. "We need to finish off the American fleet. We need to sink their remaining carriers. Only then can we assure their surrender."

He moved around the table. "We are working on a plan to draw the American carriers out of Pearl Harbor and into a trap. It's called Operation MI." He pointed to a speck of land on the large map before them. I will seek approval from the NGS to go ahead with the operation."

Fujiyama's eyebrows went up.

"So I assist Ugaki, then?"

"No. I have something else for you to plan." He handed Fujiyama a one-page handwritten note. On the piece of paper was written one word.

Alaska.

Singapore

The question of *who* and *where* the invasion fleet I sailed with was answered on the 9th of December, when news reached us that Singapore had been bombed and a Malayan invasion was imminent. As we sailed, we learned of even more war news.

In addition to Pearl Harbor being bombed on December 7th, Japanese troops had invaded British Borneo on December 16th and Hong Kong on December 18th. Luzon, in the Philippines, was invaded by our troops on December 22nd. Hong Kong fell to us on Christmas Day. Two days later, Manila was bombed and an invasion of the Dutch East Indies was mounted. At the end of January, we took Rabaul on New Britain in the Solomon Islands and proceeded to invade the largest island of Bougainville.

Our armed forces seemed *unstoppable.*

But Japan regarded Singapore as an even greater menace than Pearl Harbor. If the Japanese were to carry out their planned conquest of the East Indies, Singapore would have to be captured as well.

I joined the invasion of Malaya with other members of the press. When I reached Army Headquarters in *Kuala Lumpur,* we were told that General Tomoyuki Yamashita, commander of the crack Twenty-Fifth Army invasion force, was commanding the invasion.

I knew something about General Yamashita from his days fighting in China. He was a short, heavyset, pugnacious looking fifty-seven-year-old professional Army officer. He had a reputation for being strict and aggressive. His men called him the *Tiger*, but he would soon earn the name *Tiger of Malaya*.

Yamashita's troops were honed and ready, and given copies of a pamphlet titled *Read This Alone and the War Can Be Won*. The pamphlet recited that Westerners were weak, corrupt, and interested only in pleasure, and that they were far inferior to the Japanese. I could easily see how the Japanese would have that perception of the West—especially America. Their exposure to Western culture came from many of the movies made in Hollywood at the time. Gangster flicks and frivolous movies depicting dancing, partying, and other perceived decadences.

"The other people of the Far East look with envy upon Japan," the pamphlet went on to state. "Our opponents are much feebler than the Chinese army, and their pathetic tanks and aircraft are a collection of rattling relics."

Upon arrival at *Kuala Lumpur*, we were hurried into a sizable, official-looking building off the main thoroughfare. A military public relations officer, short and lean with dark, round glasses too big for his face, addressed us from a makeshift podium. The public relations officer kept pushing his glasses back up the bridge of his nose as he spoke. "General Yamashita's army is moving rapidly down the Malayan coast with the help of our air supremacy. The enemy is retreating before us."

As he once again adjusted his glasses, he pointed to a map of Malaya explaining our advance. We were surprised to learn that our troops bicycled down the coast roads moving twenty miles a day— more like light cavalry than infantry—with rifles and machine guns slung over their shoulders, and backpacks hung over the handlebars. If the tires went flat, they lost little time traveling on their rims instead.

The public relations officer chuckled. "We are told from captured prisoners that when they heard the clatter of our steel rims traveling down the road, the enemy fled, thinking we were hordes of tanks."

A ripple of brief laughter went through the room before he

continued. "Our illustrious troops have reached the causeway that separates the Malayan peninsula from Singapore—the British last line of defense." The officer pointed to a truck out the window. "You will all be escorted to the heights of the causeway."

The *heights* he spoke of was the Johare Straight that separated the island from the Singapore peninsula.

When we arrived, our artillery was hammering the island. I watched as observation balloons that directed the artillery fire rose high over the Straight. Not a single enemy plane appeared to attack the defenseless balloons.

We certainly did have air superiority.

I was awakened the next morning by loud explosions coming from the Straight, and it *wasn't* artillery fire. I glanced at a small calendar in my notebook in the dawn light and noted the date. February 1st.

A reporter, Genero Nakatomi, from one of the Japanese news services, burst into our tent yelling, "They're blowing up the causeway!"

"Who?" I said.

"The Brits. They're retreating," Nakatomi announced with glee.

"How does the Army get across the Straight?"

"We *already* are," Nakatomi replied. "Last night our troops landed in small boats on the island and attacked the enemy through the mangrove swamp on the other side of the Straight, which is the least obvious place the enemy thought we would attack," he said proudly. "The Brits and Aussies melted in front of our troops and deserted en masse. The island is ours!"

The battle of Malaya was over, I said to myself. *And the battle for the city of Singapore has begun.*

But it was widely known that Singapore was a well-fortified base with abundant resources for defense. The British still had the forces to attack, and rumor had it that our advancing army was quickly running out of ammunition and gasoline.

I wondered aloud what General Yamashita would do.

"That's defeatist," Nakatomi snapped. Then he sighed and caught himself. He pulled me outside behind the tent, his tone turning affable. "Look, I didn't tell you this, and if you say I did, I'll deny the hell out of it." He glanced around to ensure our conversation was between just the two of us. "I have a friend in supply. An army private. He told me that the Brits have three times the number of troops that we have."

"Three times?!"

He nodded. "This private overheard some officers arguing that a long drawn-out campaign to take the city would require far more men and supplies than we currently have. If the Brits put up any kind of determined resistance, we will run out of both ammunition and gasoline, and our attempt to occupy the city will fail."

"So will Yamashita return to the mainland and wait for supplies?"

"All I can say is, that's what he was *advised* to do by his senior supply officer."

We were both quiet for a moment before I said, "What do you think he'll do?"

The answer to my question didn't come from Nakatomi. Instead, it came from the island in the form of an immense thundering artillery barrage that went on for hours. Included in the barrage were the distinct sounds of the large wobbling shells of our new mortar weapons. Either Yamashita was crazy to allow his gunners to have an endless supply of ammunition or...

Nakatomi gestured toward the island and stated bluntly, "He's bluffing. Yamashita is bluffing the Brits."

"What?"

"Don't you see? Yamashita wants the Brits to think we've been reinforced and that we have unlimited supplies of men and ammunition."

Nakatomi was right. Yamashita was bluffing. And the bluff would not end there.

Surrender

On the 15th of February, our bombers dropped crate loads of leaflets ordering the British garrison to surrender. The next day, an entourage from General Percival's command appeared at General Yamashita's forward command post. The British officer in charge stated that General Percival wanted to speak directly with Yamashita.

It seemed British moral had collapsed.

"Come on!" Nakatomi yelled at me, shaking his hand at me impatiently. "The truck is about to leave."

I climbed onto a troop truck that was already loaded with members of the press and their gear. "Where are we going?"

"To the Ford Motor Company's assembly plant in Singapore. Nakatomi replied. "Yamashita is meeting with the British commander, General Percival."

"To surrender?"

"Don't know. And I bet neither does Yamashita," he speculated.

Inside of an hour, we arrived at the assembly plant. There stood a huge building filled with Ford cars and trucks, both fully and partially assembled, sitting on the factory floor.

Yamashita chose such a large building to house as many Japanese reporters, photographers, and newsreel cameramen as possible. He wanted to put on a show.

At six o'clock, we were led into a large conference room. In the middle stood a long metal table, where Percival and some other

British officers were already waiting. News media and members of Yamashita's staff surrounded the long table over which the two generals would meet.

Around seven that night, Yamashita finally arrived, intentionally making Percival wait for his appearance. I wondered what would happen next. Was Percival going to surrender, or was it some kind of British trick? I thought of the recent defeat of the British at Dunkirk. Perhaps Percival was trying to buy time to arrange for a Dunkirk-style evacuation, or perhaps he was waiting to mount a counter attack.

The tension in the room was palpable, a mixture of curious anticipation and uncertainty.

After some formal small talk, Yamashita and Percival got down to business. The British General addressed Yamashita and the other officers, going on and on about keeping a large contingent of British soldiers in the city to keep order.

Nakatomi nudged me and whispered, "Who's surrendering to who?"

At that point, Yamashita came right to the point. He banged his fist on the table, cutting off Percival's interpreter. "I want to hear nothing from him except *yes* or *no*."

The British interpreter asked Percival if he accepted unconditional surrender. The British general responded again about keeping a large troop contingent in the city.

Yamashita slammed the table with his fist once again and roared, "Yes or no?"

Percival replied with a simple "Yes."

I shook my head in amazement. Our German allies told us that Singapore would take several months to defeat, and it took Yamashita less than ninty days.

The suffering and deprivation of *Shonan—Enlightened South* as Singapore was renamed—did not end with surrender.

The worst was yet to come.

The following day, Yamashita's troops and tanks were paraded in front of the entire British garrison. Many of the soldiers carried white boxes filled with the ashes of fallen comrades. Yamashita commanded the victory procession to move along the main boulevard in complete silence as the British troops were forced to watch, the whole time being photographed by Japanese newsmen. A fitting end to a decisive defeat.

"Well," Nakatomi said. "Time to go to work. Dispatches need to be sent. I'm going to the city. Join me?"

I declined. "I have to get this article on the surrender finished and off to my paper." I looked at my watch. "How about two o'clock at the Cathay Hotel. You can't miss it. It's the tallest building in Singa… I mean Shonan. See you then."

After Nakatomi left, I focused my attention on finishing my article, trying to make the surrender of the *Gibraltar of the East*—as the British called Singapore—as upbeat as possible for the censors.

Sook Ching

After a quick lunch, I made my way into the conquered city to meet Nakatomi.

As I drove down a main thoroughfare, I was shocked at the scene that unfolded before me. The streets were filled with chaos. Shops were looted by both civilians and Japanese troops. Streets were littered with decomposing bodies amongst bombed out buildings. The local government had ceased to exist. Water and electricity were gone. People, young and old, looked frantically for their families in the melee.

Adding to the strain on the city itself was the increase in the population. It had swollen by the tens of thousands to unsustainable numbers by those fleeing the Japanese troops from Malaya.

I made my way through the bedlam to the area of the Cathay Hotel and parked my car. When I arrived, there were hundreds upon hundreds of Chinese in the streets surrounding the building being overseen by armed Japanese soldiers.

I worked my way through the throng searching for Nakatomi. I hoped he was in the building itself. If not, I would have a hard time finding him in the massive crowd of humanity.

Ebisu, the Japanese god for luck, smiled on me, and I found Nakatomi standing away from the mob.

"Nakatomi," I shouted. "Over here!"

I pushed my way past several British civilians who looked the worst for wear. When I reached Nakatomi, I asked him what was happening with the Chinese civilians.

He stopped scribbling in his notepad. "They're gathering them up," he said matter-of-factly.

"Why?

"A major I spoke to called it *Sook Ching,* whatever that is." He looked around at the mass of Chinese. "All I know is the local police were ordered to inform every Chinese male between the ages of fifteen and fifty to report to designated registration points throughout the island for screening."

Sook Ching sounded Chinese. Although I didn't know what it meant at the time, I would soon find out.

"Screening?" I asked.

Nakatomi nodded.

While the British troops would suffer the indignities, humiliations, and deprivations of being prisoners of war, the indigent Chinese in Singapore were about to experience the horrors of the occupier.

"Where is this major?" I asked. "I want to talk to him."

"He's inside the hotel. I'll introduce you to him."

A few minutes later, we approached two Japanese officers talking to each other. I could see from their lapels that one was a major and the other a colonel. The major was tall, lean, and buff, and wore the standard M1938 field uniform with high black leather boots.

From his armband I could tell the colonel was Kempeitai.

"Major," Nakatomi said, "We'd like to speak to you."

The major turned with a scowl, then smiled when he spotted me. "Mr. Koga. I see we meet again."

"Major Takahashi," I replied in acknowledgment.

I glanced at the colonel standing next to Takahashi. The colonel had a nasty scar that ran to the bottom of his cheek.

"And Colonel Sato," I added.

"Have we met?" Sato snapped.

"Only by reputation, sir."

"Well," Nakatomi noted. "It seems we're old friends here." His attempt at humor fell flat on both officers. "Being reporters, we hoped you could answer some questions for us."

"Major Takahashi will answer your questions," Sato said curtly and walked off.

Takahashi impatiently glanced at his watch. "So, what are your questions?"

"Why are the Chinese being told to register?" I asked.

"*Ordered* to register," Takahashi corrected.

"Okay. *Ordered.* And why only the Chinese?"

"We have been ordered to rid Singapore of all resistance to our occupation. Anyone anti-Japanese. Communists, Nationalists, members of secret societies, English speakers, school teachers, English employed civil servants, ex-soldiers, and criminals." He swept his arm over the crowd of Chinese. "And those men are at the *top* of the list."

"Why?" Nakatomi asked.

"The Singaporean Chinese supported the war effort against us. They supplied both money and men. They even fought along side the British." He looked directly at me. "I'm sure you remember China. You were there."

I barely nodded.

"We had to subdue the Chinese and eliminate any opposition, and we are *not* going to put up with any anti-Japanese elements here in Shonan."

"One last question," I said. "What does *Sook Ching* mean in Chinese?"

Takahashi leaned towards me with a barely contained smile. "It means *purge through cleansing*." He then simply laughed and walked away.

There was a tap on my shoulder, and I turned to see a young Japanese man standing behind us. "Would you like to *see* what that really means?"

He saw our reluctance and said, "You're newsmen. You want the facts, right?"

Nakatomi and I nodded our heads at the same time.

"Then come with me."

Punggol Beach

"I said to the stranger, "Who are you exactly?"

We were sitting in the semi-dark deserted balcony of the movie theater at front of the hotel.

"My name is Mamouru Shinozaki. I'm a civilian Senior Special Foreign Affairs Officer attached to the Japanese Defense HQ."

Nakatomi gave me a look before addressing Shinozaki. "That sounds a lot more official than the two of us," Nakatomi joked.

When Shinozaki failed to see the humor in the comment, I took a more serious approach. "What is this forced registration all about, and what did Takahashi mean by *purge by cleansing*?"

"Exactly that," Shinozaki replied. "Just three days after the Brits surrendered, a systematic purge of the Chinese in Singapore began." He shook his head dolefully. "If Singapore was to become part of the Greater East Asia Co-Prosperity Sphere, dissenters had to be eliminated."

"And this *screening* we heard about?" asked Nakatomi.

"The island was divided into four sections, and the commanders of the four sections were told that the screening process had to be completed by February 23rd."

He motioned outside the hotel. "That colonel you were speaking to, Colonel Sato, is Kempeitai, and he is in charge of one of the sectors."

"*Kempeitai*," whistled Nakatomi.

"Hai. They arrived in Singapore ahead of the main force. It was a garrison known as *Keibitai*, a mixture of *Kempeitai* and the *Hojo*

Kempeitai, an auxiliary military force of the 2nd Field *Kempeitai*. As soon as they arrived, they started the purge."

"How?" I asked.

"When the Chinese appeared for registration, they were inspected."

"Inspected," asked Nakatomi. "For lice or something?"

"I wish it were that mundane. The inspection methods were indiscriminate. The Kempeitai used hooded informants to identify suspected anti-Japanese Chinese. Other times, it was left up to the Japanese officers' whim and fancy. If the Chinese passed the inspection, they had EXAMINED stamped on their faces and were handed a certificate that verified that."

Shinozaki reached into his pocket and pulled out a card. "If a Chinese national was found without one of these cards in his possession...." He paused a moment. "It meant death."

Nakatomi and I were silent for a moment as we processed this information.

"And what is your part in this?" I asked.

"I've acquired several thousand of these cards and personally signed each one. I'm taking a terrible risk."

"Is this why you're telling us this?"

He seemed irritated by my question. "No. You need to see what happens to those Chinese that don't pass the inspection." He moved closer to Nakatomi and me and said despondently, "You need to report what's happening to them."

He took the card and wrote something on the back. "Go here and you'll see."

I looked at the words he wrote. *Punggol Beach.*

Purified

Our strange friend quickly departed the theater and disappeared into the crowd outside. As we returned to my vehicle, I thought, *In this horror of war, at least there are some Japanese who haven't lost their humanity.*

About a half hour out of the city, we arrived at Punggol Beach. We stopped our transport and quietly approached the isolated cove, careful not to be seen.

We found cover behind a sand dune and witnessed over a hundred Chinese civilians being forced into the surf at the gunpoint of Japanese soldiers. The Chinese had their hands tied behind their back and were instructed to stand quietly in the water.

There was a surreal moment of silence as the two different nationalities faced each other.

Suddenly, a Japanese officer barked an order and the soldiers started bayoneting the bound captives. The Chinese prisoners began to scream, and those still standing, started to run down the beach in a blind panic. The rapid burst of machine gun fire filled the air, and the Chinese were mercilessly mowed down in front of our eyes, dropping into the receding tide.

In a matter of a few minutes, every single Chinese prisoner was dead, their bodies floating in a bloody red surf. Nakatomi and I sat helpless and stunned, neither of us able to pull our eyes away from the carnage. Then he whispered to me, "Not even the dignity of a proper burial. Just have the ocean take the bodies out to sea."

We would find out later that this beach was not the only killing ground on the island. The mass killings of Chinese would go on day and night for two weeks. Tens of thousands of Chinese would be murdered, or *purified,* in the purge.

The Nationalist

While I was in Malaya and the military was celebrating their startling victories over the Brits and Americans in the Pacific, the home front back in Japan started to feel the meaning and impact of war.

Connor proved to be no exception.

Connor and Jiro had visited Kodo at the hospital where the gunshot wound in her leg was being cared for. He had told Jiro of the way Goro had abandoned his sister at the demonstration—leaving her behind to fend for herself. Jiro was angry of course, but knew there was little he could do about Goro.

Later, on a bitter cold February day in 1942, Connor made his way by bus to meet Jiro at the hospital where Kodo was to be released, her leg finally healing. As Connor rode toward the hospital, he saw military training taking place in an open public park. These military exercises were now performed openly and on a daily basis after the attack on Pearl Harbor.

As he arrived near his stop, the streets were jammed with soldiers practicing street fighting and lugging heavy machine guns from one location to the next. A crowd of curious Japanese watched these maneuvers from the sidewalk and cheered with patriotism.

Connor had become dispirited by the incident with Kodo, and decided to stay away from the Yakuza.

But it would not be as easy as he believed.

His thoughts were interrupted when he was brashly pushed

aside by a tall, lean man dressed in the dull khaki national uniform, wearing a field cap similar to the ones worn by the Army. The man pushed Connor so hard that he stumbled into the muddy gutter.

"Ijin!" he snarled, glaring down at Connor with dark piercing eyes while placing his hand on the handle of a ceremonial knife strapped to his belt.

The nationalist, his face twisted with hate, loomed over Connor when a voice came from behind.

"Connor-san!"

Connor looked up and saw Jiro and Kodo walking briskly towards him.

There were now three against one, but what really shook the nationalist's confidence was *Kodo*. Though she was a woman, he recognized her as Yakuza. That was a reputation he didn't want to tamper with, so he gave Connor one final glare before quickly leaving and blending into the crowd.

"You shouldn't be on the street, Ijin," Jiro remarked. "If you haven't noticed, Americans are not very popular right now."

Connor didn't argue the point.

"It's good to see you, Connor-san," Kodo grinned. "Forget about that kusoyarou." She moved very close to Connor and forcefully pulled him to her. "How about we celebrate my recovery," she said with a devious smile.

Home Front

In the days after Pearl Harbor, an air of uncertainty in the nation hung heavy in the air. It was hard to believe Japan had entered a war with the West. Rationing, which had begun slowly in 1939, was expanded not only to include gasoline, coal, and telephones, but also sugar, charcoal, and matches. Sake was no longer made from rice, but sweet potatoes and acorns.

When Connor entered his house, he noticed Kenji and Suki munching on a roll. "Sweet buns?" he asked in surprise.

Standing next to Miyoko in the kitchen was Mrs. Ito, the old lady who owned the tobacco store down the street from the Fujiyama's and who headed the local neighborhood association.

"To celebrate the fall of Singapore," Mrs. Ito said and pointed to the buns on the table.

As Connor quickly claimed his share of the treats, he noticed the water buckets and the makeshift broom made from a bamboo rod and bundle of rope standing in the corner of the kitchen. The rope was to be doused in water and used to beat out flames. In addition, every household was required to keep a bucket of water on the front step and four small sacks filled with sand, all of which were used to put out fires.

Mrs. Ito noticed Connor's scrutiny of the buckets and broom. "We cannot be too careful. We must be ready for any air raid. The drills now are once a month." She looked around the house and said to Miyoko. "You have your blackout curtains?"

Miyoko nodded. "We are ready. And thank you for the sweet buns. Both the children and I enjoy them," Miyoko said to change the subject. Talk of air raid drills upset her.

"Now, off to school with you, Kenji," Miyoko said. "And Suki, go get your comfort bags and give them to Mrs. Ito."

She smiled at Connor. "And you, Connor. Please try and stay off the streets."

Resistance

Since the incident with the Yakuza, the bullies had kept their distance from Kenji. Now he could enjoy going to school without the fear of being taunted and tormented.

Pearl Harbor had changed the daily activities at Kenji's school as well. Like all the schools, daily air raid drills were practiced, and regular displays of patriotism were also a part of the daily routine.

These tests of patriotism made Kenji uncomfortable, especially since they were directed at Japan's enemies, one of which was America.

On one particular day, Kenji found himself confronted with an extremely uncomfortable test where his streak of independence would ultimately land him in trouble.

His class was sitting in front of the school's principal, an elderly man, standing stiff and erect with a streak of martial attitude in his eyes, when he asked, "Let's say that an American flag is placed here," he pointed to the wooden floor at his feet. "You are all walking towards it. What would you do?"

"Trample it!" the class shouted in unison.

All but Kenji.

The principle noted Kenji's silence. "What about you? What would you do?"

"I would bow deeply as I pass by," the young boy replied.

His reply was followed by a thunderous denunciation from the classroom.

The principal bristled and snapped sternly, "Come with me Fujiyama."

He didn't give Kenji time to stand. Instead, he grabbed the boy by the arm and led him to his office.

Warnings

As Miyoko entered Kenji's school, she hoped it was a simple discipline problem, but down deep she feared something worse. Had he once again shamed his family with his fondness for Western culture?

In these desperate times, it didn't take much for the prying eyes of the secret police or dangerous rumors brought forth from members of the Neighborhood Association to bring suspicion upon the family. Even a misspoken or misinterpreted word could bring dire consequences.

With the National Mobilization Law established on December 8th of 1941, virtually anyone in Japan was liable for arrest for any thought or action considered unpatriotic. Simply having a foreign paper in your possession or discussing war news that appeared in the daily papers, could be cause for arrest.

Just last week, Mr. Izumi, whose son was killed in the China War, was arrested and jailed for merely saying, *"However much one may speak of the nation, can a parent help but weep?"*

Miyoko wiped those thought from her mind and entered the principal's office where Kenji was seated, looking as if he had been severely reprimanded.

She was told of Kenji's offense and cautioned about how her children should be taught at home.

Miyoko, shaken by the accusation, bowed and apologized for her young son and promised that it would never happen again.

The principal seemed to ignore her vow, and instead, wrote something down in his ledger. He then dismissed both mother and son with a wave of his hand.

Once at home, Miyoko begged Kenji to be more discreet with his comments and actions. "Kenji. Please understand. These are dire times," she said. "Dangerous times, and you must be careful not to provoke the establishment for it could have serious consequences, not only for yourself, but for our entire family as well."

"But they wouldn't dare harm my father," Kenji replied confidently. He confidence was quickly dashed by the look of fear on his mother's face.

Kenji, feeling a sense of dejection and frustration for being punished due to his admiration of American culture, went to his room and slid his door closed. He retrieved a short-range radio from under his bed and tuned it to the British radio station he frequently monitored to learn of the war news.

Radio broadcasting was under the control of a single organization, the Broadcasting Corporation of Japan, and radios were to be tuned *only* to those Japanese stations. This policy was tightly controlled. Every household was forced to make a list of all radios in their possession, and short-range radios were strictly prohibited.

Kenji had received his radio from his school friend, Black Patch, who had a knack for building them. His friend was called Black Patch because of the dark brown birthmark that covered almost a quarter of his face.

Kenji began listening to some jazz music when he heard raised voices coming from the living room. He peaked out his door and his spine turned to ice. Standing there with his mother and sister was a stout man wearing a green uniform, black boots, and leggings.

Tokkō.

He quickly turned the radio set off and stuffed it under his bed.

That done, he walked down the hallway to the living room and eavesdropped on the heated conversation.

"Your blackout curtains are not correct. I can see light coming from your window," the Tokkō officer stated. "You must correct this immediately."

Miyoko bowed and apologized politely. "Where is the light coming from?"

"Come. I'll show you." He led Miyoko and Suki outside to the back of the house. "There," he said, pointing to a small tear in the blackout curtains.

It was almost invisible, and not worth mentioning, but Miyoko immediately feared the real reason for the Tokkō's visit.

"And while I'm here, I will need to check your house for radios," he said.

The policeman began to search the house, room-by-room, inch-by-inch. After he found only one in the kitchen, he stared at Miyoko. "I will have to take this with me to have it checked. Short-wave reception is illegal."

Miyoko watched the man's eyes glance at Kenji, who huddled in the hallway. "Boy, are there any more in this house?"

"Ie," Miyoko replied. "That's the only one."

The policeman yanked the cord from the wall and without so much as a thank you, turned and marched out of the house.

When Fujiyama returned home an hour later, Miyoko sat with Kenji and Suki, and told her husband of the incident at school with Kenji and the visit from the Tokkō.

Fujiyama shook his head and addressed his young son. "Kenji, you place yourself in too much danger. And our family, too."

Fujiyama knew that Kenji's radio could bring the Tokkō, or worse, into their lives, but he too wanted to hear news that the government did not want anyone to discover. "Please keep that radio out of sight and the volume turned down."

"Yes, sir," he smiled.

Miyoko grabbed her husband's hand. "The visit from the Tokkō was based on such trivial grounds. They are sending us a warning."

"Ie," Fujiyama replied. "Not a warning but a *message*. To me. I'm being watched."

A Chance Meeting

While unease haunted every corner of the Fujiyama household, a distraught Hiyakawa spent the first couple of weeks after Pearl Harbor detained in the Japanese Consulate in Honolulu with others of the diplomatic corps waiting in the same internment status.

The virtual black out of communications and diplomatic relationship with Tokyo prevented Hiyakawa from obtaining any information on his wife. His every waking moment was consumed with fearing the worst, and when able to sleep for a few restless hours, he dreamed of his wife's desperate plight.

In late January 1942, he and the other Japanese diplomats, along with their families, were ferried by military plane to Los Angeles and then to Union Station. But it quickly became clear that Los Angeles would not to be their final destination.

It was a gray and blustery day, and while waiting with the others, Hiyakawa witnessed a distressing sight. Huddled together on a platform on the other side of the Union Station tracks were clusters of Japanese-American families. Though he could guess why they were there, he still walked over to one of the Military Police guarding his group to inquire about the situation.

"Those families are being sent to internment camps," the broad-shouldered corporal grumbled. "For their protection." Then he added with a tone of irony. "And ours."

"But they're Americans," Hiyakawa protested.

The corporal only shrugged. "Get back with the others," he said, abruptly ending the conversation.

While they waited on the platform, Hiyakawa approached the group of Japanese-Americans, noticing they all wore thin paper nametags that rattled in the breeze.

As he moved closer to them, he wondered what could he say to comfort them. His country's thirst for war had put these American citizens in their present situation. He felt racked with guilt and personally responsible for their plight.

He started to turn away when he noticed the nametags of a couple that sat alone with their belongings.

It read *Koga*.

Could it be?

He walked over to the couple, excused myself and asked, "I couldn't help noticing your nametag. Do you have a son in Japan named Yoshihara?"

When they heard Yoshihara's name, their dispirited mood lifted, and their faces brightened.

"You know our son?" Mr. Koga asked.

"Is he well?" asked Mrs. Koga anxiously.

"Yes. He's fine." Hiyakawa looked at the poor victims before him and shook his head. "I'm so sorry for all this."

Mr. Koga nodded. "Yoshihara tried to warn us when he was here last year. But we would not, *could not*, believe him."

"When will you see my son again?" asked Mrs. Koga.

"I don't know. I don't even know when or if I will be able to return to Japan."

When a tear came to Mrs. Koga's eye, she wiped it softly and gently squeezed Hiyakawa's arm. "When you do see him, tell him that we are okay. We are strong and doing well."

A whistle blast screeched from across the platform as a train approached the station. "If I do see Yoshihara, I will give him your love," Hiyakawa said.

"Hai. Domo," they both responded.

Hiyakawa rejoined the group just as his train pulled into the platform. They were ordered aboard and soon were headed far from Japan and his beloved wife to parts unknown.

"So vast. So large," Hiyakawa noted to Consul General Nagao Kita sitting beside him, as the vast landscape of America passed by their windows on the journey to the East. "How could we be so foolish? How could we ever believe we could defeat such a large enemy?"

Kita nodded. "Yamamoto was right. The only way to defeat America is to dictate terms of surrender in the White House," he sighed, gazing out at the passing landscape of small farms, towns and villages.

"Have they told you where they are taking us?" Hiyakawa asked. "How will we be treated?"

"I've been told that it will be better than those poor Japanese-Americans we saw back in Los Angeles." He flicked an errant fly from his sleeve. "Under the terms of the Geneva Convention of 1929, the United States is bound to protect our diplomats and their families. So they are interning us in a resort until we can be repatriated."

"A resort?"

Kita nodded. "Hai. First class accommodations. We'll remain there while exchange arrangements are made."

"What of the other Japanese caught in the U.S. when Pearl Harbor was bombed?" Hiyakawa asked. "The businessmen and other professionals?"

Kita was quiet for a moment before responding. "We will press to have them reciprocated first, of course."

Hiyakawa, having lived with an American wife, knew the term *reciprocated* would be a matter of some contention. "You will have problems with the Americans."

When Kita chose not to respond, Hiyakawa moved on. "What's the name of our resort?"

"Montreat. In the mountains of North Carolina. We'll be treated well during our stay in hopes their diplomatic officials will receive similar treatment." He leaned back in his seat. "Hopefully we can be exchanged soon and be sent back to Japan."

"How soon?" Hiyakawa asked anxiously. "I have to locate my wife."

"I don't know, Hiyakawa. I just don't know."

Both men turned and stared out at the passing countryside, alone with their thoughts and concerns.

Bataan

"We haven't moved in days," Kuro said between mouthfuls of his meager breakfast rations of dried fish and rice. "All we do is send out patrols."

"Hai," grunted Taka. "I thought the Americans were melting away from our attacks. I don't understand why we are not moving forward?"

Yoshi swirled the green tea in his cup. "A captain told me that our Army had suffered many casualties. Perhaps we are waiting for reinforcements."

Kuro scoffed at the notion. "It's already the first of April. How much longer do we wait?"

Kuro's question was answered by a gruff voice behind them. "Get up," Sergeant Gunso barked. "We've been ordered on another patrol."

Taka looked at the sergeant with an expression of doubt.

"We have been ordered to scout out the base of those mountains," the sergeant replied, pointing to his left.

Within the hour, Yoshi's platoon pulled their gear together and followed their sergeant toward the mist-covered mountains that loomed in the distance. Walking through the waist-high lemon grass, Yoshi alternately took turns wiping the beads of sweat from his forehead and swatting flies that seemed intent on entering his nostrils.

And it was hot. *Very hot.*

Yoshi was walking in a daze, and it was all he could do to keep himself from fainting. But he was abruptly snapped out of his mild stupor when the grass around him started to shake with the sound of a sickle slicing through the glade.

"*Down, down!*" Gunso ordered.

At the same instant, a soldier to Yoshi's left howled in agony. Yoshi looked and saw the young man's intestines spill out onto the ground, his body nearly cut in half by the rapid stream of machine gun fire. The gutted man stood there for a bizarre moment in time, as if the state of his body hadn't yet caught up to his brain, before falling forward and crumpling to the ground.

Yoshi fought the urge to vomit while he pressed his frame into the earth—and under it if he could. Soon, he was nearly run over by two soldiers lugging heavy machine guns. The soldiers quickly set up their weapons next to Yoshi and began firing in concert with rifle fire from others from his platoon.

Yoshi lifted his head cautiously and moved into position to join in the refrain of fire when everything abruptly stopped.

"Everyone up," came the gruff voice of Gunso from the front. "Keep moving!"

"I didn't see a thing," Taka said, acting disappointed as he approached Yoshi. "Typical of cowardly Americans." He turned to Kuro. "How about you? Kill any of them?"

Kuro shook his head.

"Enough talking," Gunso snapped. "Keep moving." The words had barely left his lips when what started as a hint of a whistling noise over the platoon's heads, quickly turned into a loud roar of artillery fire.

Again the platoon dropped to the ground, keeping their heads down and faces pressed into the dirt. But the shells fell short and then once again, silence.

These intermittent, ineffective artillery attacks recurred for the remainder of the day, but fortunately, they suffered no casualties from enemy cannon fire.

Eventually, Yoshi's first day turned to night on Bataan.

That evening, the platoon began to load into a fleet of military trucks.

"Where are we going?" Kuro asked.

"The brigade has been reinforced, and we are going over the mountains," Gunso replied as he walked up to the truck. "The Americans anchored the end of their defensive line in the mountains, but since they consider the rugged terrain impassable, they did not extend their forces far up its slopes." He eyed his men one-by-one. "And we will make them pay for that mistake."

The convoy trucks, with their lights switched off, navigated over narrowly constructed paths down the mountain and through a dense forest. When the procession stopped, the troops exited the trucks and took up positions as directed by the company commander, Captain Ikeda. Ikeda was about forty years of age, had a dark complexion, and wore glasses above a mouth of protruding teeth. As a veteran of the war in China, his vast experience comforted the young recruits.

Yoshi joined Taka and Kuro in a foxhole and offered them some stale rice. "It's quiet," he remarked to no one in particular.

The other two nodded their heads.

Just then, two soldiers—one tall and thin, the other built like a freezer—approached. They pushed a khaki-uniformed soldier before them.

Taka raised his rifle and challenged them.

"Stand down," the tall soldier commanded. "We have a POW." Taka saw that the prisoner of war was a Filipino. "What are you going to do with him?"

The squat private replied, "Unlike you, our machine gun squad has a shortage of personnel." He poked the Filipino soldier in the back with his rifle. "We need someone to carry our ammo box."

The Filipino corporal stared down at his boots.

The tall private grabbed the Filipino prisoner by the neck. "You understand? You've been liberated from American bondage by the Japanese Army."

The prisoner looked up at the scrawny private, shook his head and replied defiantly in English, "No." Then the man spat on the private's feet.

"Dirty pig. You should be shot," the stout private shouted. He looked to the other private, who stood there undecided.

Then, from Yoshi's side, a shot rang out, and the prisoner clutched his stomach before falling to the ground, writhing in agony.

All eyes went to Taka, who cradled his rifle to his shoulder. Taka stepped closer to the fallen Filipino, pressed the barrel to the man's forehead, and fired again.

Yoshi stood frozen in his spot, his mind reeling from Taka's brutal, cold-blooded actions. Before he had the chance to speak or even really process what he had just witnessed, orders came down for them to move out once again.

The next day dawned, and Yoshi and his company found themselves at the base of the mountains surrounded by thick jungle as far as the eye could see. Various species of birds sang from the trees, but the pleasant sounds gave no relief from the scorching sun and fierce heat of Bataan.

"I feel like I'm in a sauna," Kuro remarked. "Let's find an open path."

"How many times have you been warned to stay away from them?" Sergeant Gunso grunted. "The enemy is waiting for you with machine guns. An entire squad was annihilated on one of those paths just the other day."

As they hacked their way through the jungle, Yoshi could hardly believe how dense it was—much different than the *Tarzan* movies he saw in America. There were few trees, and instead, bushes and bamboo groves covered with vines grew massive and unchecked.

The unique Bataan bamboo groves were almost impossible to cut through and slowed them down considerably. And the vines proved painful as well. They dug into the men's exposed flesh and were difficult to remove without tearing open the skin.

During their trek, Yoshi and his platoon had passed several points where U.S. Forces had previously camped. Yoshi found himself impressed with the camps. There was no trace of human waste anywhere. The sites were all extremely clean and hygienic—so much different from their camps that were full of filth and feces.

By the afternoon, with the glaring hot sun pounding on Yoshi's head, the platoon arrived at a river approximately forty meters in width. The water in the river looked clear and cool and seemed to call to Yoshi and his fellow comrades. Yoshi stared at the water wanting desperately to strip down and plunge into the inviting liquid.

Before taking action on this impulse, Yoshi noticed several Filipino soldiers lying dead, face down in the water, halfway across the river. The corpses were severely bloated and their uniforms were the only thing that held together the rotting liquid of their bodies.

Suddenly, a fusillade of gunfire erupted from the jungle on the other side of the river. Machine gun bullets ripped past their heads.

The entire platoon with Yoshi, Taka, and Kuro in the lead, sprinted across the river. Bullets peppered the water around them, and Yoshi prayed he would be spared.

When the three young men reached the other side of the waterway, they jumped into a dugout carved into the mud and rocks as ear-piercing explosions rained down all around them. The heat in the makeshift shelter felt like a moist cellar, and an unpleasant odor assaulted them.

The dugout, once used by the enemy as a machine gun emplacement, was covered with heavy planking and sandbags, but was also was filled with the smell of death—swollen corpses of dead Americans surrounded the men and their feet stood ankle deep in a thick ooze of water, mud, blood, and excrement.

Yoshi's heart thrashed wildly in his ears, and he felt suffocated by the tight confinement and stink of the bunker.

The artillery shells landed closer and closer. Huge plumes of river water shot into the sky behind them. Yoshi looked up to see dozens of his platoon struggling to cross the river, most of them being ripped to pieces by the barrage of shrapnel.

Yoshi, Kuro, and Taka pressed themselves deeper in the vile mud beneath them as shells began to fall closer. The concussion of the shells rattled their teeth, and dirt and debris toppled in from the top of the dugout.

Suddenly, Kuro stood up, sheer terror filling his eyes, and he attempted to climb out of the dugout. He scrambled over the sandbags and planks in panic and ran directly toward the jungle.

"Stop!" Yoshi pleaded, but as soon as the words left his lips, an explosion turned over the earth in front of Kuro, tossing the young boy into the air like a child's toy.

When the dust finally cleared, Taka and Yoshi heard a low moan in front of them.

"He needs help," cried Yoshi. He looked over at Taka, who huddled in the corner, frozen in fear. "We have to help him," Yoshi pleaded, but Taka just stared ahead with blank eyes.

"Damn it, Taka!" Yoshi yelled, but knew it was useless. He climbed out of the bunker and headed for his wounded comrade.

Yoshi's feet pounded over the dirt. He couldn't believe what he was doing. Shells exploded around him, pelting him with dirt and rock, but he fought through the chaos and finally made it to Kuro's side.

Though Kuro was badly wounded; he was still alive.

"Help me, *Okasama*. Help me."

Yoshi patted his arm. Captain Ikeda had told Yoshi that many soldiers, when seriously wounded in battle, pleaded for their mother—*Okasama*.

Yoshi looked over his fallen war comrade. Shell fragments had ripped into his right arm and leg, and blood streamed down to his hands and feet.

He was about to help Kuro to his feet when he noticed a glint of sunlight in the corner of his eye—an enemy soldier was coming straight at him—the bayonet on the tip of his rifle gleaming in the sun. American or Filipino, he didn't know. His attention was fixated on the advancing bayonet.

Yoshi quickly brought his rifle up but the enemy soldier thrust it aside with such force that it flew from Yoshi's hands. The soldier—a Filipino—moved to impale Yoshi, but the young private instinctively reacted with his martial arts training learned from his father. He grabbed the front of his opponent's rifle then fell onto his back.

The Filipino soldier was momentarily shocked and lost his balance, falling towards Yoshi and over on his back. Yoshi grabbed his bayonet from its scabbard, scrambled to his knees, and thrust it into the soldier's neck.

Yoshi stood there for a moment, dazed, slowly realizing he had just killed a man.

The moment of bitter victory didn't last long. Another enemy soldier came running out of the jungle, yelling and cursing something in Filipino. Yoshi took a stance with the bayonet in his hand, ready to take on the new threat, but the enemy soldier stopped and took aim.

Yoshi raised his bayonet as if to ward off the bullets that were surely headed his way—a useless act, he knew.

But Kuro hobbled to his feet, turning his body toward the enemy soldier just as he fired. The bullet tore through Kuro's back.

The enemy soldier tried firing again, but his rifle jammed. He dropped his rifle and reached for his sidearm.

With little time to think, Yoshi threw himself at his enemy. They fought fiercely, hand to hand, for several moments, until Yoshi managed to grab his opponent's pistol and empty its magazine into his enemy at close range.

Yoshi sucked for air, exhausted from the ordeal. He looked around for Kuro, but his search was short lived. Out of the jungle, came yet another enemy soldier, walking slowly, taking dead aim at him.

Yoshi responded with the pistol but it was spent.

Three words went through his head. *I am dead.*

Yoshi flinched as shots were fired, but it was the enemy soldier who fell to the ground in a heap. Yoshi looked over to see Kuro crouched on the ground, clutching Yoshi's rifle.

Yoshi sighed in relief, then assisted his wounded friend to his feet. The shelling had thankfully stopped, and Yoshi dragged his friend back to the bunker.

Yoshi gave Taka a cold stare and said, "The least you could do is help me get him to the field hospital."

Taka's face reddened in shame, then he nodded obediently and the three young men began to make their way back across the river as a sudden downpour of warm rain fell down from the gray sky.

A Pyrrhic Victory

It took almost an hour slogging through the jungle for Yoshi and Taka to carry Kuro, who came in and out of consciousness, to reach the field hospital. Once there, they arrived upon an unnerving scene. Severely and mortally wounded soldiers were all around them. Men with bloody stumps for arms and legs screamed upon their stretchers. They looked exhausted and gaunt, revealing the fierceness of battle.

And the smell! The toxic fumes in the hospital tent reeked of blood, ether, and gangrene assaulted their senses.

"Corporal," Yoshi said to a young medic bent over a wounded soldier. "My friend here is hurt. What..."

"Over there," the medic replied abruptly, without looking back at Yoshi. He pointed to an area filled with wounded soldiers.

Yoshi and Taka carried Kuro to the distressing scene and laid him gently to the ground. They set their rifles down and sat next to him.

Yoshi pulled out his canteen—his throat on fire from thirst—and guzzled the refreshing water. The number of wounded and dying men surrounding them was unimaginable.

This is the honor that Taka was so fond of?

He reached down and took Kuro's hand and immediately felt how stone cold his friend's skin appeared. He knew before even looking at Kuro's face that his comrade was dead.

Before he could mourn the loss of his friend, a soldier was thrown to the ground in front of them by a sergeant. The soldier landed on a bandaged wrist and howled in pain.

"Leave the coward be," the sergeant ordered. "He shot himself in the hand to get out of combat."

The private whimpered pathetically, clutching his bandaged wrist to his chest.

The sergeant's eyes burned as he stared down at the wounded soldier. "He should be shot for his cowardice." The sergeant then turned his attention to Yoshi and Taka. "And what about you two? Why are you here? If you're not injured, return to your unit at once."

Yoshi and Taka didn't have the fortitude to challenge the sergeant. Instead, they took one last look at their dead friend, then walked away, left with no other choice but to return to their unit.

"It's over," shouted a soldier to Yoshi and Taka as they rejoined their unit. "The Americans have surrendered!"

Yoshi felt an immediate sense of relief that the fighting had finally ended. He had survived combat and survived it honorably. But his moment of silent celebration was short lived when a thought struck him. *But I have lost a friend.*

What was left of his platoon had no time to enjoy the news of the American surrender. They were told to move out, and within hours, they found themselves on a main road crowded with all manner of Japanese Army vehicles. The dust kicked up by the caravan and the dragging feet of thousands of POWs and refugees was stifling.

Through the dust and the intense heat, Yoshi could see groups of a thousand U.S. and Filipino soldiers, guarded by only twenty Japanese soldiers marching along the road in a long, serpentine line. Their faces were blistered from the sun and covered with dust and filth making them look years older than they were. Combat had turned these young boys into old men.

They look like the walking dead, Yoshi thought.

Fallen bodies of POWs that had either died or were too weak to continue, were left behind, and the vehicles rolled over them without mercy.

A young Japanese officer, with no apparent reason or provocation, grabbed a POW and pushed him off the road, tied him to a tree, and used him for bayonet practice.

Yoshi winced as each thrust sliced into the poor man's body, his screams for compassion falling on deaf ears.

Yoshi looked back over his shoulder and watched civilian refugees mingle with the columns of POWs. The large procession of humanity seemed to go on endlessly.

Taka, his bravado returned, sidled up to Yoshi and bragged, "Look at them. Look at the weak Americans. They were easy to beat."

Yoshi turned on Taka and unleashed his frustration on the young man. "And at what price? Our friend Kuro's death? For your *honor*?"

Taka had no answer. He kept silent.

A hand suddenly grabbed Yoshi from behind. "You two," a young officer growled. "Put bayonets on your rifles and come with me."

The two young men followed the officer towards the line of POWs marching along the road. "Keep them moving. Poke them with your bayonets. Stop for nothing," the officer instructed them.

The officer's attention then turned on three American POWs who sat on the side of the road. The American's had blank stares on their faces and looked completely spent. "Get those *Gaijin* on their feet," he roared to no one in particular.

Yoshi watched as two Japanese soldiers ran over to the Americans and began to ruthlessly kick and strike them with the butt of their rifles. When the men were beaten to unconsciousness, one of the soldiers began to strip the prisoners of their watches and rings. One of the prisoner's rings refused to come off. Yoshi watched in horror as the Japanese private proceeded to cut the American's finger off with his bayonet, then left it behind like a piece of garbage.

A Filipino prisoner came over to bind his comrade's bloodied stump, but was beaten back with the butt of the soldier's rifle. The Filipino prisoner fell into the road and Yoshi watched as a truck swerved deliberately out of its way to run the man over. Several other trucks followed suit, crushing the prisoner's body until little more than a bloody stain remained on the dirt road.

Yoshi was aghast at the brutality he was seeing. *Is this the honor and glory we were taught in training?*

A hand shoved him from the rear. "Stop standing around and gawking. Guard those prisoners," an officer ordered.

Once again, Yoshi and Taka followed orders and walked to the line of prisoners that trudged down the road. They came to two American soldiers lying facedown in the road. A Japanese soldier stood over the motionless bodies.

The soldier kicked at the prisoners and shouted in Japanese for them to get up. When the Americans didn't respond, the soldier bayoneted one of them in the back then looked over at Yoshi and gave him a half-smile. "Your turn."

Yoshi looked at his fellow countryman, then at the prisoners, and then finally at the officer standing across the road watching and waiting. He glanced at the bayonet attached to his rifle and began to tremble and sweat.

"Kill him," the officer screamed at him.

Yoshi stared down at the American. A young, blond, boyish American that looked a lot like Connor.

Kill or be court-martialed.

He was jarred from of his dark thoughts when Taka stepped forward and thrust his bayonet into the American's back. Taka repeated this act again and again, until Yoshi grabbed his arm to stop the brutality.

"Private," snarled the officer. He withdrew his service sword and walked towards Yoshi. "You are a coward," he snarled.

"He is not a coward," a voice roared as Captain Soji Okada approached and glared at the officer. "This soldier has been awarded a medal for bravery—*and* been promoted for it."

"But *I* am a lieutenant, and he disobeyed my direct order," the young officer countered.

"And I'm a *Captain*, Lieutenant. Leave the boy be." As the young

Lieutenant relented and stood down, Okada smiled to Yoshi. "Private, or should I say, *Corporal,* come with me."

What Price Honor

As Okada and Yoshi approached headquarters in the Captain's vehicle a half hour later, Okada noticed Yoshi's mood.

"Aren't you happy with your promotion? You've been given two weeks leave to return home."

Yoshi attempted to smile, but failed miserable. "I can't believe our Army would actually act in such a brutal manner. The POWs are treated like—animals."

They both were silent for a moment, then Okada spoke. "It's the Bushido code," he finally said. "By surrendering, the POWs have lost all honor and loyalty to their beliefs. A warrior, a *Samurai*, was to commit suicide rather than surrender. The example held up by today's militarists of Kusunoki Masashige in the 14th century—committing suicide when the cause is lost. So, an enemy who surrenders is held in contempt. And is therefore seen as less than human."

"I know. We were taught that in training. The Field Service Code."

"Correct," the Captain replied. "*Don't live and be put to shame as a prisoner. Death will not incur the sin of dishonor.*"

Yoshi nodded. "A soldier gives his life in duty to the Emperor. But I never thought it would lead to the practice of such barbarism."

Okada exhaled and nodded.

Yoshi noticed his Captain's dispirited reaction. "Is this the real meaning of the Bushido code, sir?"

Okada paused a beat. "There was once a fine military code of

Bushido that consisted of five main tenets. But now, the code has been corrupted."

"How?" asked Yoshi.

"Righteousness, courage, humanity, propriety, and sincerity. Those were the main tenets of Bushido. Bushido in this original form did not condone cruelty."

Yoshi was quiet for a while as they drove further from the nightmare he had experienced. "I don't know if I could take my own life, sir."

"*Gyokusai,*" Okada said. "Taking one's life needlessly."

"Hai," Yoshi replied.

Okada gazed down the road as if to see the future. "I'm afraid that ideology of wanton suicide is going to lead to something far worse for our nation. For our soldiers. For our young men. Perhaps even for our people."

Yoshi did not understand what Okada meant.

Okada patted the young man on the shoulder. "Let's hope it never comes to that." He pointed to a sprawling command post looming in the near distance. "We're here. Soon, you're going home."

Chian Iji

I was sitting with Nakatomi at our regular table in the Cathay Hotel restaurant, organizing notes for my next report when he said, "Amazing. Japan has seized in several *months* what took the colonial powers several *centuries* to acquire—one million square miles with one hundred and fifty million people."

I raised my head and replied, "Hai. Quite a feat." I could not share Nakatomi's enthusiasm, nor could I fake enthusiasm.

I'd seen the horrors of Nanking, but that was during a battle. Though the battle of Singapore was over, the true terror had just begun. The purges of Singapore did not end with its surrender. I could not believe what I had seen after the fall of Singapore.

In the weeks following the purge, the Kempeitai continued to instill fear amongst the city's residents. Its name became synonymous with cruelty, terror, and death.

After I shared my disgust with Nakatomi, he simply shrugged, "*Chian iji.* The maintenance of order."

I shook my head. "Does that *order* include torture and the use of criminals as enforcers?"

"The Kempeitai use what they can. Can you fault them for that?"

I was about to answer when we heard a commotion outside the window of the restaurant.

A group of Japanese solders were standing on the sidewalk, jeering at something. But it was difficult to see what they were shouting at as the crowd blocked our view.

Thinking a possible story was in the making, we left the restaurant to see what the commotion was all about. Outside, in the middle of the street, a large group of POWs huddled together as they were paraded along for all to see.

"I thought all POWs had been rounded up after the battle."

"Could have been hiding in the city," Nakatomi suggested.

I noticed that the POWS—mainly British—were sickly and severely emaciated, so much so they could hardly stand. But that didn't stop the column of guards on either side of the prisoners from beating them if they slowed down or fell to the ground.

I had enough. "I'm going back into the hotel."

As we turned, a group of civilians in front of us—British and Chinese—were on their knees, bowed, with their faces pressed to the pavement. A few moments later we saw why.

A Kempeitai colonel and his aides were walking towards the civilians. I recognized the colonel immediately.

"Colonel Sato," I said respectfully as he approached.

His scarred faced narrowed, and his eyebrows rose in unison. "Koga. Correct?"

"Yes, sir," I replied.

"Getting enough material for your newspaper?"

"I could always use some more."

"Good. Come with me. Both of you." He smiled that hideous grin. "I'll show you what we do with terrorists and traitors here in Singapore."

We took two separate vehicles to the old YMCA building in the East District Branch that the Kempeitai used as a prison. The closer we got to the prison the more Nakatomi became agitated.

"What's wrong?" I asked. "Why so nervous?"

"Haven't you heard what the Kempeitai do at that prison?"

"Rumors only."

"I, for one, don't know if I have the stomach for it."

After a twenty-minute ride, we arrived at the YMCA building and were escorted by Sato's aides through the main doors and down into the stifling hot basement of the makeshift prison. We walked by filthy cells filled with filthy prisoners. I noticed in one cell, a bowl of some indefinable material that I assumed was food sat in the middle of the floor.

Suddenly, human screams came echoing down the hall from somewhere in front of us.

One of our Kempeitai aides nudged me and smiled. "That could be either eardrum piercing, fingers breaking, or a simple beating," he said smugly.

The other aide chimed in. "I disagree. It's probably electric shock."

They both laughed at their little disagreement.

Nakatomi and I, on the other hand, were not amused.

We walked up a flight of stairs leaving the revulsion of the cells behind. At the top, Sato was waiting for us.

"Come," he said. "I'll show you how we interrogate political agitators." He directed us to a large room, its floor covered in urine and feces.

Nakatomi and I promptly covered our noses.

Noticing our attempt to block out both the odor, Sato laughed with delight. He led us to an anteroom, and there lay a Chinese man face down on a table, naked from the waist down—massive bloody welts covered his buttocks and legs. A Kempeitai sergeant stood over the prisoner's limp body holding a frayed stick of bamboo.

"This nice young man is telling us who his fellow agitators are," Sato said smugly. "Watch."

Nakatomi and I winced as the sergeant hit the poor man over and over again, eliciting shrieks of pain and pleas for mercy.

Sato noticed our reaction. "We Kempeitai believe that torture can be very therapeutic."

My hatred for this animal of a man grew in an instant. I couldn't believe the callousness that he so easily and appallingly espoused, as if sadism was the most natural thing in the world.

I knew what Sato was *really* doing, though. This was no favor to a reporter looking for a story. No, this was a blatant warning for my occupation to toe the line and to witness first-hand what the Kempeitai were capable of.

The lesson was not wasted on either Nakatomi or myself. But the lesson was not over yet. Sato wanted to make sure we truly understood what was at stake.

He led us out of the building and onto a basketball court. There, we saw three men tied to makeshift polls that had been buried in the ground. Their faces twitched and bodies trembled.

Several Japanese soldiers stood in a rigid line on the basketball court, the tips of their bayonets quivered as they awaited a command. The line of soldiers looked pretty raw to me. Probably new recruits sent in as replacements—untested in battle.

"These men are spies," Sato pointed to the wretches tied to the stakes. "But they can still serve the Empire." He turned to a major who I had become quite familiar with in Manchuria. *Major Takahashi.*

Sato gave Takahashi a nod, and the major barked an order to the young soldiers.

Up until then, bayonet practice was merely on dummies made from straw. But now, the recruits had to stab an actual human being for the first time.

"Do not stab in the red circle," Takahashi voice boomed.

I looked over and saw that each of the prisoners had a red circle drawn on their chests. I didn't notice it before. "That's the heart. The only place you are prohibited to strike," Takahashi uttered. "Understood?"

"My god, they're going to keep them alive for bayonet practice," Nakatomi whispered.

And he was right. We watched as the recruits, one after the other, obeyed Takahashi's command and repeatedly took turns stabbing the staked prisoners, careful not to touch the red circles.

I couldn't watch it anymore, but didn't dare turn away. Sato was not watching the sordid spectacle. He was watching us. When all that was left of the prisoners were a bloody bag of bones, Sato dismissed us. "You may leave now."

One of the Kempeitai grabbed our arms and ushered us out the back gate and onto the street.

I knew not exactly what Nakatomi was feeling at this point, but as for me, my alienation from my maternal country became complete. I was filled with hate for those who had driven a gentle and cultured country into war and for those who have used it for their sadistic purposes in the name of a superior race.

I vowed to bring down this inhumane system somehow, no matter what the cost.

Hailstorm

When I arrived in Tokyo, the first thing I did was call ahead to see if Fujiyama was in Hiroshima. His aide informed me that he was indeed in Hiroshima, but he had been deep in strategy meetings for the last week or so and that he could only take messages.

My guess was something big was brewing. Something bad.

I arrived at his home on the eighteenth of April in hopes he could convince my editor to assign me to the Imperial Navy, and away from the revulsion of the Army. But instead of arriving at the end of a family celebration, I walked into a hailstorm.

The first thing I heard emanating from the kitchen was someone screaming, "Defeatist!"

A cloud of tension hung over the kitchen as Hiryo shouted at Yoshi. "All this talk is defeatist," he said as he paced the floor. "The enemy is cowardly and morally weak. We destroyed their Navy at Pearl Harbor. We defeated them in the Philippines and drove the British out of Singapore."

Connor watched as Fujiyama attempted to act as an intermediary between his two paternal sons as I entered the kitchen.

"Perhaps I should leave," I volunteered, seeing the clear discourse in the family between the two brothers.

"No, please stay. We're just having a discussion over the war," Fujiyama said calmly. "And Japan's execution of it.

Hiryo turned his attention to me, hoping for an ally. "You've seen it with your own eyes. My father says you were a war correspondent in China and Singapore. So, you've seen the superior spirit of the Japanese, correct?"

As Fujiyama nudged me, I could see why he wanted me to stay. My initial instinct was to avoid entering into a family disagreement, but my negative war experiences over the last year drove me to respond bluntly to the young fighter pilot.

"I think the chances of Japan winning the war are slim."

"*What?!*" Hiryo shouted.

"Let him speak, Hiryo," Fujiyama commanded. "Not only is he a guest in our house but, as you have rightly pointed out, Yoshihara has seen the war up close and personal."

Hiryo reluctantly conceded and plopped down at the kitchen table.

I took a breath and continued. "Hai. Our military has won amazing victories against the British and Americans. But our chances of winning this war are not guaranteed. If not for moral reasons, then for the myth instilled by the government that the spiritual power of the Japanese makes us superior to all other peoples." I waved my hand for emphasis. "Spirit is not enough to win a war against enemies that far outnumber us *and* whose ability to make war far surpasses that of Japan."

Hiryo stiffened, but I was not done yet.

"The Japan I knew from my parents, a land of kind and gentle people with the traditional morals of the Samurai, seems to have disappeared—at least in military and government circles." I lowered my voice and looked directly at Hiryo. "I feel like a stranger in my maternal land."

Yoshi pointed a finger at Hiryo. "And I've seen what Mr. Koga is saying. *You* haven't seen the brutality of our military. You fight a sanitized war from thousands of feet in the air!"

Hiryo brooded silently.

Yoshi paused for a moment to collect his words. "I for one don't believe our military is practicing the true code of the Samurai."

This piqued Connor's interest. He hadn't heard criticism of the Samurai code from any one of the Fujiyama's before.

"Righteousness, courage, humanity, propriety, and sincerity. Those were the main tenets of Bushido from which the Samurai code was derived," Yoshi stated, parroting the words of his commanding officer, Okada. "The Samurai code did not condone cruelty. The military has made the code into a travesty."

But Hiryo was not moved in the least. He grumbled something under his breath and stormed out of the house.

I looked at Connor to gauge his reaction to the argument, and he appeared genuinely confused.

Fujiyama touched my arm. "Let's go into the living room."

When we were seated on the low cushions, he motioned toward the kitchen. "I know you didn't come here to be involved in a political discussion. Probably the *last* thing you wanted."

That was putting it mildly. "I came to ask you a favor." I went on to explain my revulsion of the Army and to see if he could put a good word in for me with my editor and have me assigned as a war correspondent with the Imperial Navy.

"Without giving away any military secrets, I think I can convince your editor that something extremely newsworthy will be generated by the Navy very soon."

He poured himself a cup of sake that was sitting on the low table and offered me one. After the heated discussion, we both could use a drink.

"Now then, I have a favor to ask *you*," he said. "Though your interaction with Connor has been brief, I know he likes you. You are the only American here in Japan in his life. I would like you to talk to Connor. He's having a hard time here. He feels out of place, and quite frankly, I don't blame him. It's not enough that the Japanese do not see him as one of their own, even though he is a formal member of my family, but now that the war has started with America..."

"And me having a foot in both worlds," I added. "I'd be happy to talk to him."

"Thank you," Fujiyama said, then excused himself.

A few beats later, Connor walked in with my host.

"Connor," Fujiyama said, "Yoshihara would like a word with you." He patted his son on the back and once again left the room.

There was a long pause of silence until I spoke up. "Your father says you're having a bad time of it here in Japan."

"Japan or America. Same difference." His tone and body language oozed bitterness. "I just don't fit in."

"You heard what I had to say to Hiryo in the kitchen?"

The young boy nodded.

"I would say our alienation is in reverse," I offered. "You're an American wanting to be Japanese, and I am Japanese wanting to be American."

That caught Connor's attention. "You *want* to be an American? Why?"

I drained my sake before answering the young man's question. "I left the U.S. because of the bigotry towards Japanese-Americans thinking I would find a better home here in Japan."

I paused a moment to phrase my thoughts. "But I quickly found that my prospects in Japan were dim, and the image of my country was even dimmer. But I know now I would rather be a Japanese-American, than just Japanese."

The sound of air raid sirens abruptly interrupted our conversation when Fujiyama burst into the room, his face drained of color as if glimpsing death first hand. "Tokyo is being bombed!"

The Raid

The day stood clear and sunny as Miyoko walked through the small park across from the military hospital. The shadows from the bare limbs of trees cast a melancholy mood over the commons, but that didn't deter an old man from sitting on a bench, picking out a chirpy song on his shamisen. Across from him, a small gathering of men and women practiced Shinjitai. Their slow, thoughtful movements complimented the beauty of the park.

Miyoko bowed to the group respectfully as she passed and soaked in the serenity of the early morning. Her quiet thoughts were abruptly halted by the sound of loud airplane engines roaring above her. She and the others in the park stopped their activities and gazed skyward as three medium-sized twin-engine bombers flew so low to the ground that they shook the trees and the ground under Miyoko's feet.

As the lumbering planes passed overhead, general bewilderment gave way to cheers from the park residents. Those in the park, Miyoko included, assumed they were Japanese planes.

That assumption was put to rest just moments later.

The receding sound of the engines was replaced by a high-pitched whistling sound. Miyoko looked back over her shoulder to see a group of small black objects dropping from the bellies of the planes.

Before she could completely comprehend the scene, she was knocked off her feet by the blast of a numbing shock wave. She sat on the ground, confused and dazed, gazing through a haze of consciousness at the people around her running in blind panic.

She regained her composure and stood up on wobbly legs, only to feel tiny pinpricks pepper her face and arms. Without warning, debris of small shards of metal and chunks of concrete rained down upon her.

In an instant, she lay in the dirt, bleeding and unconscious.

Lost

Upon hearing the news of Miyoko's injury, Fujiyama gathered up his family and arrived at the hospital by train that afternoon. The cross that flew over the building that was once a Catholic hospital had been removed, and in its place stood a red East Asia flag.

The family immediately found the doctor in charge of Miyoko's care. Yoshi, Hiryo, Kenji, Connor, and Suki all asked a million questions about her condition at the same time.

"Hai. She is doing fine. In good spirits as well," the doctor reassured them. "Minor cuts and bruises on her face and arms, and a good sized gash on her head. Nothing life threatening, but we'd like to keep her here awhile for observation."

"Can we see her now?" the entire family asked, almost in unison.

The family stayed with Miyoko all afternoon and through the evening. But because of what was being called by the American radio broadcasts *the Doolittle Raid*, Yoshi and Hiryo were immediately recalled from their leave, and they left late that night.

The radio broadcast announced the surprising details of the attack, concluding that the raiders came from a secret base called Shangri-La. But the General Staff knew the low flying B-25 bombers of the U.S. Army Air Force somehow took off from aircraft carriers off the coast of Japan.

Fujiyama could only marvel at the American's audacity. As

Yamamoto speculated, America was not going to lie down and surrender anytime soon.

Being a high-ranking Naval officer, Fujiyama was granted the appropriate consideration, and he along with Connor and Kenji, was given quarters in an empty bay for the evening.

The next morning, after eating a light breakfast of barely digestible hospital food, Fujiyama announced his plans to his family. "Suki will stay here with your mother. Connor, Kenji and I will return to Hiroshima this evening. In this state of emergency, I'm pressed to return to my headquarters as quickly as possible."

Connor wanted to remain there with Suki, but Fujiyama said it was not a good idea being around Japanese since the bombing. So that evening, at the end of a day of pouring rain, Fujiyama kissed his wife, and he and his two sons headed for the Kobe train station for the return trip to Hiroshima.

Settling into their compartment, all three were trapped within their own thoughts. The rain settled into a light drizzle, and small drops of precipitation populated the compartment's window that Connor gazed through. The dark and dreary landscape matched his mood. He was worried sick over his adopted mother and was surprised at the level of anger he had with the American pilots that attempted to harm her.

Unable to answer his own silent questions, Connor turned to Fujiyama. "Didn't they know their attack would injure civilians? Or was it deliberate like the radio broadcast said? Did the Americans actually intend to bomb hospitals and schools."

"You can't believe everything the government says," Fujiyama replied, closing the newspaper he was reading.

"The hospital was near the factory they bombed. Unfortunately, there's always collateral damage in war."

That didn't make Connor feel any less angry. Americans almost killed his adopted mother, and he didn't understand Fujiyama's offhand attitude. Why wasn't he cursing the Americans? Connor was about to challenge him on that when the train unexpectedly slowed.

"Why are we stopping?" asked Kenji.

"Wait here," Fujiyama replied and abruptly left the car.

When the train finally came to a halt, the boys exchanged a knowing look. Then they both stood and went to investigate. They exited the train and joined other curious passengers pacing along the tracks. The night was cold and damp, and the train stood perched with a narrow strip of rocky ground to their right and a treacherous hill to the left. The sound of rushing water echoed from the darkness below.

As the curious procession of passengers trekked along the tracks, an engineer approached. "Everyone, please go back to the train," he ordered. "There's a mud slide ahead covering the tracks. It's not safe. Return to your cars."

Connor was about to take Kenji back to the train, when the ground shuttered underneath his feet. Connor suspected the worst. "Back to the train," Connor shouted. Having lived in Los Angeles, Connor feared what might happen next, and shoved Kenji towards an open train door. But as quick as Connor reacted, it was too late. The earth below their feet rumbled and shook so violently that it tossed them to the muddy ground.

Connor managed to regain his balance, yank Kenji to his feet, and drag him to the open door. But the mass of other passengers had the very same intent. Men and women shoved past the two boys, and Kenji was knocked towards the edge of the narrow precipice.

"Help me," he screamed amidst the crush of the passengers.

Connor pushed his way through the scrambling crowd just as the earth below Kenji's feet gave way into a mudslide. He made a final surge toward Kenji and managed to grab onto a small sapling. In a single motion he pulled Kenji off the receding ground.

Kenji landed face first in the shaking mud. His eyes filled with tears as he looked at Connor. "Thanks, brother."

The celebration was short lived. The sapling that Connor clung onto, gave way under his weight, its roots pulled from the soil and he slid off the precipice and into the dark night below.

A Forward Defense

Over the next couple of weeks, authorities searched for any trace of Connor, but to no avail. The Fujiyama family mourned his loss but refused to think their adopted child was gone forever. Out of respect for his wife, Fujiyama held off telling Miyoko about Connor until she was released from the hospital.

Upon hearing the news, and although she respected her husband's rationale, Miyoko was stunned and spiraled into a deep depression. It was left up to Kenji and Suki to help Miyoko through her mourning as Fujiyama had additional concerns on his mind.

Stunned, too, was the nation. The Doolittle Raiders not only bombed Tokyo and Kobe, but Yokohama, Nagoya and other cities, throwing the Naval General Staff into a panic, even though the raids ultimately caused very little damage.

"In a way, Admiral," Matome Ugaki, Yamamoto's Chief of Staff, noted, "the bold raid by the Americans proves your point, sir. We must destroy the carriers of the American Navy and push back our defensive borders far beyond their ability to attack the homeland again."

His planning staff, including Fujiyama, had assembled in Yamamoto's office on a dull, grey morning on the battleship *Nagato* in Hiroshima Bay.

Yamamoto, sitting behind his metal desk, replied stoically, "I told that to the NGS. I explained to them Operation MI, the invasion of Midway. I told them Midway was part of a forward defense line running from New Guinea through the Solomon, Gilbert, and Marshall Islands, Wake, Midway and the Aleutians."

"And...? Fujiyama asked.

"Being as conservative as ever," he replied, "they believe we were stretching our forces too thin with the Coral Sea operation beginning shortly. I assured them we had sufficient forces for both."

"I agree," stated Ugaki, who perused the operation's plan for Midway. "We will outnumber the Americans two-to-one in carriers and planes, and they can field no battleships."

"So is Midway a go, sir?" asked Fujiyama.

Yamamoto stood up from his desk and approached the map of the Pacific. "Hai." He looked at Fujiyama. "And our diversionary attack in the Aleutians should keep Nimitz's attention away from Midway until it is too late.

"When Nimitz realizes our target is Midway," Ugaki added confidently, "he will have to send his remaining carriers to its defense and be obliterated in the process."

"Oi. Let us hope so," Yamamoto replied. "Finish up the details of Operation MI and report to me this evening."

As the staff filed from the office, Fujiyama pulled Yamamoto aside. "The NGS could very well be right. MI is a complex and risky operation."

"Are you saying I'm playing poker?"

Fujiyama laughed. "You're known for it. In my opinion, sir, you plan most of our battles according to poker strategy and percentage play."

Yamamoto bellowed that deep laugh of his. "Oi. But if we can destroy the remaining American carriers, there is nothing standing between the American West Coast and us. We can bring this war to a quick, merciful end."

Fujiyama nodded and gathered up his papers when Yamamoto asked, "I heard about your American boy. Any word?"

"No. Nothing."

Yamamoto searched for the right words of condolences, but they eluded him. "Well, those American pilots that were shot down are going to stand trial and possibly be hanged."

"But they are prisoners of war."

"Certain quarters are looking for ways to salvage their honor. The Emperor's life was endangered with the bombing of Tokyo. A price has to be paid." He hesitated then said, "I'm sorry for you and your family, but it is not a good time to be an American in Japan."

Fujiyama understood what he meant. And as sad as it was, perhaps Connor might be in a better place.

Arrested

Connor stumbled his way through the countryside before finding himself standing in the middle of a dry rice paddy, where he finally collapsed from utter exhaustion.

After being washed up onto the muddy banks of the creek, Connor had wandered through the uninhabited countryside for days. The vicious blows to his head suffered during his fall and the subsequent beating through the raging river water had left him dazed and confused. He had tried to orient himself, but was only rewarded with flashes of memory of who he was and where he came from.

Now, he sprawled in the rice paddy, pressed his eyes closed, and clutched at his head. A severe ringing pounded in his ears, and he heard voices, real or imagined, that floated through his semi-consciousness. One voice in particular repeated itself time and time again, demanding to be answered.

The voice was in Japanese, followed by a blunt object poking him on the shoulder. At first it was just a prod, but then a realization of pain shot rippled throughout his body.

"Get up, pilot," the voice demanded.

Connor finally opened his eyes. A blurry image of a farmer stood over him. The man gripped a pitchfork. He stabbed Connor again. "Up!"

Connor screamed in pain as the pitchfork punctured his thigh. He reached up and tried to grab at the instrument of his torture, but he could barely make out his tormentor, let alone seize the pitchfork.

Suddenly, someone behind him lifted the young teen off the ground and forced him to his feet.

Connor cried out hoarsely as his weight pressed onto his bleeding leg.

"American pilot! Name?"

Connor glimpsed behind him and spotted another man. This man was different than the farmer. Tall and elderly. A home guard soldier. The man shook Connor and screamed at him again in Japanese.

"American pilot! Name?"

Connor forced his mind to compute his situation, but all his voice could muster were sporadic words in Japanese.

"I...Japanese...home...father...Japanese..."

"He's crazy," the farmer declared, thrusting his pitchfork at Connor once again.

"Enough," the old soldier barked. "Follow me," he ordered, and the two men dragged Connor out of the rice paddy and toward a small home in the near distance.

A New Assignment

"**W**ho do you know in high places?" growled my editor, Tomoko Sakura, his ever-present cigar clenched between his teeth.

"What do you mean?" I asked.

Sakura waved an official looking piece of paper in his hand. "I have here an authorization for you to join the Imperial Navy as a war correspondent."

I smiled. Fujiyama had fulfilled his promise. "That's good news."

"Oi," Sakura shook his head. "I'd be sick of the Army bullshit, too." He sat down on the edge of his desk. "Maybe the Navy will let us print more of the truth about whatever hell hole you're crawling into next."

I didn't necessarily believe that, but anything was better than the horrors of the Army.

"You're to report to the base at the Naval Arsenal in Yokosuka and board the light carrier *Shoho.*"

A carrier! What luck!

"And where is it destined to?"

"Not sure. But it says to dress for the Nan'yo—the South Seas." He grinned a wide Edward G. Robinson smile around his cigar. "Better bring your flippers." He shuffled through his desk searching for something. "I don't know where you're going, so I have no background information for you—only what I have on the *Shoho.*" He handed me a thin portfolio. "Good luck and keep your head down. I don't want one of my best reporters turning up dead."

"Not the best of pep talks, but I'll try my best."

After a short cab ride to the arsenal, I showed my authorization to the guards and boarded the *Shoho*. With suitcase, typewriter, and portfolio in hand, I was soon escorted to my quarters. They were much more comfortable than anything the Army had ever provided. I settled in for a comfortable night's sleep and chased away thoughts of the dirty land war I had experienced.

The next morning at breakfast, I sat with the other war correspondents assigned to the ship. I was about to take a sip of my tea, when a hand slapped me on the back.

"Yoshihara!"

I turned to see the smiling face of Genero Nakatomi, my colleague in Singapore. "You here, too?" I asked.

He plopped down next to me, stirring his cup of tea. "Couldn't stomach Singapore and the Army *victories* any longer. Begged to be reassigned, and this is where I ended up." As Nakatomi dispensed with the small talk, he moved onto more pertinent conversation. "So, what rumors have you heard? Do you now where we're going?"

I shook my head. "Your guess is as good as mine." But I knew he had heard something. "But I'm sure *you* know."

"Only our next destination." He lowered his voice. "The big naval base at Truk. It's a couple hundred kilometres northeast of New Guinea."

"And..." I asked, raising an eyebrow.

"*And* we're suppose to join a large naval task force there."

"And then where?"

"Don't know," he smiled. "But it should be fun."

I was silent a moment then said, "You know, there's no place to hide on the ocean."

Nakatomi knew what I meant. Unlike China and Singapore, this battle would offer no shelter or protection.

We arrived in Truk at the end of April and soon thereafter were joined by four cruisers and one destroyer. I walked the flight deck one night, contemplating what an ocean surface battle would be like. I knew enough in conversations with Fujiyama that carriers were going to be prime targets in this new war.

I attempted to chase that troubling thought out of my mind so I could enjoy being out on the vast, wooden deck, feeling the warm breeze blowing around me. It was much better than the humid atmosphere in the cabins below.

"Get a sun tan later," Nakatomi said as he approached. "They're ready for the briefing."

A few minutes later, a half-dozen war correspondents were huddled in front of a Navy public relations officer dressed in class-A whites. He stood in front of a large map of New Guinea and the Coral Sea.

"Shinshi," he began, "The High Command, has decided to continue our expansion into the Nan'yo for the glory of the Emperor and the Empire." He pointed to a spot on the large map behind him. "Our forces have continued down the Indonesian island chain, and have overrun most of New Guinea. But American and Australian troops have managed to hold the southeastern part of the island centered on the Australian administrative capital of Port Moresby. If we seize all of New Guinea, communications between the United States and Australia will be cut off, and Australia will be knocked out of the war."

He turned back to his audience of reporters. "So, the objective of this operation is Port Moresby on the southern end of British New Guinea." He pointed again to the map. "Port Moresby is necessary as a base from which to launch an invasion of Australia."

A low buzz spread around the room.

Australia.

The public relations officer ignored the clamoring and continued with his briefing. "The *Shoho* and its support ships, under the command of Rear Admiral Aritomo Goto, will provide air cover for the invasion of Tulagi. We will use Tulagi as a support base to cover our flank and provide reconnaissance support for our naval forces advancing on Port Moresby. Once accomplishing that assignment, the *Shoho* will join the main invasion force towards Port Moresby."

He glanced around the room. "Any questions?"

Several of the reporters wanted to know more details of the operation, but were told to be patient. "You will know soon enough."

Meanwhile, I wondered why we were extending battle zones to far-away places. Did we have enough materials to wage such a war effectively?

Little did I know at the time, the answers to these questions would come a mere two years later.

Discovered

In the early morning of the May 4th, the day after the successful invasion of Tulagi, the task force was at anchor in the bay. I was seated in the mess hall of the *Shoho,* eating breakfast with Nakatomi.

"Piece of cake," he said.

"No thanks," I replied.

"No. I meant the invasion. *Piece of cake.* Easily done."

I shrugged my shoulders. I'd come to expect our military to succeed at pretty much anything these days, and I was about to state that fact when a klaxon alarm blared in our ears.

We rushed out of the mess hall and onto the deck just in time to see dive-bombers attack the large minelayer *Okinoshima.* The *Okinoshima* and two destroyers were positioned to provide a protective barrier for cargo ships unloading troops and materials.

"Those are *American* carrier planes," Nakatomi said. "Where did they come from? And how did the Americans even know we were here?"

We watched in morbid fascination as bombs rained down on the ships around the *Okinoshima,* sending tall plumes of water erupting into the sky. But just as fast as the attack began, it ended, with the American dive-bombers and torpedo planes being chased to the south by our Zeros.

Even though there was smoke emanating from the *Okinoshima,* the damage to the ship appeared minor.

"What do you think?" Nakatomi asked as we felt the *Shoho* weigh anchor, preparing to leave port with the other ships.

"I think the Americans are smarter than we thought. I also think the invasion of Port Moresby isn't going to be as easy as that public affairs officer claims."

A couple of days later, I was in my cabin typing up my report of the invasion thus far. I believed Fujiyama to be right. This was going to be primarily a carrier war. For the first time, the surface ships would never engage directly with one another.

I put that speculation in my report, knowing that such analysis on my part would keep me in good standing with Sakura and the newspaper. Sakura could print my speculations as popular analysis for our readers without having to worry about censors. After all, if this were really going to be a carrier war, then Japan would surely win it.

I was just putting the finishing touches on my prognostications when the now familiar call to battle stations came blasting throughout the ship.

I was out of my cabin in a flash, nearly running over Nakatomi whose face carried the sense of danger upon us.

"Enemy bombers," he shouted. "They're attacking the ship!"

We made it to the flight deck but were immediately ordered below deck by a petty officer. "Get inside. Can't you see we're launching planes?"

Just as the words left his mouth, a Mitsubishi Zero roared past us, mere feet from where we stood. The blast from its engine knocked us back inside.

As soon as we scrambled back to our feet, Nakatomi wasted no time. "Follow me," he yelled as he shouldered his camera bag.

The *Shoho* had no observation and command structure on its flight deck, so Nakatomi led us to an open portion of the bow. From this open-air position, we saw a scene both exhilarating and perilous at the same time. Bombs exploded around the ship, sending white, foamy columns of water into the air.

"Those are American B-17 Flying Fortresses," he observed. "Land based. Probably from Port Moresby." He looked around the ship. "Their bombs fell wide. Nowhere near us."

"That's not good," I said watching our attacking fighters take off after the B-17s.

"Not good? But they *missed*."

"No. I meant, we were found."

Coral Sea

On the morning of May 7th, that realization spread amongst everyone on board the *Shoho*. We were in harms way, knowing that at least one American carrier was in the area.

The *Shoho* steamed toward Misima Island in the Coral Sea, when two of our combat patrol planes intercepted American carrier planes. We hardly had time to put on our life jackets when a gunner manning an anti-aircraft gun pointed toward the sky and screamed, "Dive-bomber!"

He swung his gun around and fired. The booming of the gun painted the sky above us with puffs of black anti-aircraft fire. Pieces of flak danced around the dive-bomber, but could not stop the inevitable. Through ebony clouds of flak, the enemy plane dove towards us, joined by a shrieking sound I had become quite familiar with.

"Down!" I yelled toward Nakatomi, but my warning was not necessary. He was already hugging the metal deck, and I quickly joined him.

The shrieking of a falling bomb abruptly ceased, and we heard a deafening explosion somewhere below us. Then, as if some giant hand had reached down from the heavens and grabbed the ship, the *Shoho* shook violently, sending vibrations throughout the entire vessel.

We regained our footing and climbed the stairs to the flight deck just as a second explosion rocked the compromised ship. This mighty blast was followed by several larger explosions.

We attempted to reach the flight deck, only to be forced back by a fireball charging towards us. We were thrown back into the anti-aircraft gun position, our hair and eyebrows singed from the intense heat.

"That came from the direction of the hangar," Nakatomi screamed. "Bombs must have past the flight deck, and ignited the fuel and ammunition in the hangar. We have to..." He stopped, looked out over the ocean and froze.

I followed his eyes and saw the source of his horror. A thin, white line of wake headed towards the ship. We both knew at once what approached.

Torpedoes.

Moments later, the lethal spars slammed into the side of the ship directly below us. A deadly fusion of steaming hot ocean water, metal shards, and fire hurtled towards us in an instant. Everything went silent as we were tossed around like rag dolls, falling overboard and into the boiling brine below.

I had no way of knowing how long I floated unconscious in my life jacket, but when I regained some semblance of awareness, I peered through foggy vision as the *Shoho*, stern first, quietly sank into the boiling sea.

My stomach sunk along with it, and a wave of nausea surged over me. I heard the screams of my fellow countrymen being consumed by flaming oil. I was helpless to assist them and could only imagine their agony.

I searched the surface of the water for our other ships, convinced they would most certainly be looking for survivors. It only took me a moment to realize there were no other ships, and the survivors were alone in the water. The rest of the fleet must have left the area to escape attack.

Was I to die here in the ocean? Was this to be my fate?

As I bobbed along the surface of the water, I could make out a solitary lifeboat drifting my way. I treaded water the best I could and waited for the lifeboat to reach me. Finally, after what felt like hours, the boat brushed past me, and I grabbed at the ropes hanging from its sides with my right hand. But when I reached for the side of the lifeboat with my left hand, I screamed in agony.

I hadn't realized it before as I drifted in the water, but my left arm had swollen to three times its normal size, and I feared it broken.

I struggled to pull myself into the lifeboat with only one good arm and fought to push away the pain radiating from my left—finally pulling my sodden body into the boat.

I looked around to behold a horrifying sight—the eyes from a severely charred body stared back at me.

It was Nakatomi.

"*Yoshihara*," he moaned. "*Help me...*"

"I'll do my best, my friend," I grunted through the pain. "I'll get you through this." But I knew without rescue, both our chances for survival were slim to none.

Prison

When Connor opened his eyes, he wore a moist towel on his chest, and a pan of hot water stood next to his rickety bunk. He looked up at a petite, middle-aged, Caucasian woman, who sat beside him. The woman was dressed in a sack dress that came down past her knees. As Connor gazed at the woman, an odd thought crossed his mind. *If she wore make-up, she would look more attractive.*

He tried to pull himself off the bunk when the woman softly implored, "No. You must rest. You still have a touch of fever."

Connor attempted to speak, but his voice was still too weak.

"You've been sick," she said. "For a few weeks. We thought it was pneumonia, but it turned out to be some kind of simple infection." She patted him on the arm. "You're much better now."

Connor looked into her eyes. "*You* took care of me the whole time? Who are you?"

"My name is Barbara Hiyakawa. And you?"

He cleared his throat, still feeling rundown and weak. "Connor. Connor Fujiyama."

Barbara's eyes opened wide. "You are the American boy that Commander Fujiyama adopted?"

"Yes. How did you know?"

"My husband, Kenta Hiyakawa, told me about you and how Fujiyama took you into his family."

Connor vaguely remembered the name Hiyakawa. A diplomat, he thought. "Where are we exactly?"

"This," pointing around her cell, "is the Sugamo prison for political enemies and POWs. The prison is in the suburbs near Tokyo."

"*You're* a political enemy?"

She nodded sadly before asking, "And how did *you* get here?"

Connor went on to explain his mother's hospital visit in Kobe, the train ride on the way back to Hiroshima, the earthquake, and nearly drowning in a raging creek.

"I was found by a farmer who thought I was one of the downed pilots from the Doolittle Raid." He pointed to his filthy clothing covered in brown mud. "I guess my jacket must have looked like a bomber pilot's."

Barbara stood up. "We need to get you out of here and back home," she said with unwavering determination. "I'll talk to the guards."

Several minutes passed, and Connor hoped his nightmare was about to end when the door opened, and Barbara returned with a gruff looking Japanese civilian.

"This boy belongs with his Japanese family," she said in a firm voice. "He should not be here. He needs to be sent home."

Niko Kimura, known as Little Glass Eye, was a stout, disheveled-looking man, not much taller than Barbara. After losing his left eye in China, Niko was relieved of service.

Now he was a paid civilian guard at the prison.

Little Glass Eye walked up to Connor, and after several seconds of scrutinizing the American boy, he decided upon a course of action. He abruptly swung around at Barbara and punched her square in the face.

His brutal blow sent the woman sprawling across the floor with such force that her simple tunic rose above her thighs, exposing the scars and bruises of prior beatings.

Connor was appalled by what he witnessed, but before he could say anything, Little Glass Eye lifted him off the make-shift bed by his neck and slammed him against the cell wall.

"To the kitchen," he growled, and pushed Connor out of the cell, leaving Barbara squirming and moaning on the rancid floor.

Political Prisoners

"What has Mrs. Hiyakawa done to deserve this kind of treatment?" Connor asked, wiping the tears from his eyes. "I saw scars and bruises on her legs."

Mrs. Kent, once a social worker in Yokohama, stood next to the boy in a filthy kitchen preparing foul-smelling vegetables. "She has been branded an enemy of the nation," Mrs. Kent replied stoically.

Connor watched as the woman cut onions that were black with rot. "What happened to her hair?"

"Hacked off with garden shears by the soldiers," she said. "A form of humiliation. But she wears it proudly. She is defiant and that doesn't help her case here."

"Who else is here at this prison?"

"Mostly British and Dutch women." She lowered her head. "It's been difficult for us," she said. "We lost most of our personal belongings, our beautiful and carefully kept homes, our servants, nannies—our jobs."

"All of you are political prisoners?" Connor asked.

Mrs. Kent snorted. "All it takes is a single misinterpreted word and you are branded a spy or worse from the Tokkō or Kempeitai."

"Barbara said there were POWs here."

"Yes. Transients. Picked up after Pearl Harbor. I think they were captured in the Philippines. They're on their way to work camps." She touched Connor on the hand. "And I fear that may be your fate as well."

She put down her cutting knife. "I need to attend to one of the wounded POWs." She handed Connor a bag of mango beans. "Look through these and sort out the little black bugs the best you can. We'll make a dinner of soup from the beans tonight."

It took Connor a few hours of tedious work to separate the rancid bugs from the mango beans. When he finished this task, he set out to find Barbara.

As he returned to the cellblock, he heard a frantic voice echo down the concrete hallway. "No! I won't let you. You're not taking this girl."

As Connor turned the corner, he spotted Barbara standing in front of a young Caucasian girl, no more than thirteen, who clung to Barbara for protection.

"I have orders," yelled Little Glass Eye. "She's to work for Nippon!" The golden haired girl whimpered as Little Glass Eye snatched her by the arm.

Barbara immediately slapped Little Glass Eye's hand aside and shoved him into one of the bunks. "She's not going to be one of your prostitutes. I won't allow it."

Little Glass Eye stumbled back to his feet, his face flushed with rage. He threw himself at Barbara, punched her face several times, causing her to lose her grip on the young girl.

He grabbed the terrified girl by her blonde hair, lifted her from the concrete floor and began to drag her out of the cell.

Connor, seeing Barbara face down on the cold concrete floor, lurched at little Glass Eye but was quickly dispatched by a blow to his head from the stout guard that sent Connor careening across the cell.

Despite a bloodied nose and lips, Barbara rose to her feet and attempted to yank the young girl from Little Glass Eye's grasp. She was rewarded once again with a severe blow to her head that left her writhing on the floor.

As Little Glass Eye loomed over the young girl, ready to strike, a tall Japanese sergeant entered the cell.

"What's going on here?" he commanded.

Little Glass Eye looked up at the sergeant, his face transforming from anger to fear in an instant. "This girl has been ordered to be a comfort woman."

"By whose orders?" the sergeant demanded.

Before Little Glass Eye could respond, Barbara stood, wiping the blood from her face. "He has no such orders. He wants her for himself."

The sergeant glared over at Little Glass Eye. "Only the Army makes those orders. Leave her be."

Little Glass Eye backed away from the girl who raced over to Barbara and buried her head once again in her side.

The sergeant motioned to the gash that leaked over Barbara's eye. "You need to have that looked at."

As Little Glass Eye exited the cell, he leveled a deadly look at Barbara that turned her blood cold.

For His Sake

"Do you think it's wise, sir, for you to lead the invasion force against Midway?" Fujiyama proposed as he tried to maintain his balance in the Captain's dinghy that plowed through Hiroshima Bay.

The waters of the bay were extremely treacherous the first days of May 1942, due to a late winter storm brewing off the coast. Yamamoto and his staff had moved the Admiral's flagship to the *Yamato* in preparation for the Midway invasion.

Yamamoto stiffened from the question. "I want to be near this operation. Midway is crucially important to the Americans as a vital outpost of Pearl Harbor. We must destroy the American carriers when they respond to our invasion."

Fujiyama knew what Yamamoto meant about being close to the operation. Nagumo was once again to lead the carrier attack force against Midway. His mission was to neutralize its defenses in preparation for Yamamoto's invasion force, and Yamamoto was leaving nothing to chance—not even Nagumo.

"But the Coral Sea operation was a tactical victory, sir," Vice-Admiral Ugaki piped in.

"A tactical victory, yes." Fujiyama replied. "Strategic, *no*." He looked at the report that he clutched in his hands. "We lost one light carrier and one line carrier."

"But the Americans lost two of their line carriers," Ugaki replied. "We sunk the *Lexington* and seriously damaged the *Yorktown*. It would be a miracle if they are able bring her back to Pearl Harbor.

And even if it did return safely, the American Navy cannot match us carrier for carrier. We already have a two-to-one advantage over them."

"Hai. Even though the American Navy is reluctant to be drawn into an all-out battle, they managed to prevent us from mounting an invasion of Australia. Admiral Inouye was so unnerved by the loss of our carriers," Yamamoto snapped, "that he ordered the Port Moresby invasion to be canceled and the troop transports to turn about and get out of harm's way." He looked around at each officer. "*That* is why we need to destroy the American carriers with one final crushing blow."

The sun set over the bay with a fiery blaze of orange as Fujiyama and Yamamoto paced the deck of the *Yamato* in silence.

The storm had subsided, and the gentle sound of waves slapping against the hull of the great ship was the only noticeable sound they could hear around them.

Yamamoto finally broke the silence. "A young pilot came to me just before our Coral Sea operation. He confided in me his fear of us losing the war."

Fujiyama was shocked at hearing a statement by his commanding officer that was tantamount to defeatism. "That was either very brave or very foolish of him."

"Perhaps. But I've known him and his family for quite some time, and they knew my feelings on our country going to war." He watched as the sun slipped past the horizon. "He was still a boy, really. Killed at the Coral Sea," Yamamoto said quietly. Then his resolute mindset returned. "We must win at Midway. For that young pilot's sake if nothing else."

Bad Luck

Hiryo had just landed his Mitsubishi A6M2 Zero fighter on the deck of the *Akagi* and was immediately ordered to report to the Squadron Commander. But first, he wanted to find Fuchida.

He stopped a fellow pilot and asked of his friend's whereabouts.

"He's in the infirmary," the pilot answered. "Appendicitis."

"No!" Hiryo said, and rushed to the infirmary. When he arrived, Fuchida was sitting up in bed.

"How are you, sir?"

"Better," Fuchida said with a grimace. "I should return to my duties shortly, but I will not be flying."

"But we need you to lead the attack force over Midway," Hiryo protested. "Just like Pearl Harbor."

Fuchida smiled. "No. Not I. *You're* going to lead a squadron in the attack force—Lieutenant Commander Fujiyama"

"But sir..." He stopped short. "*Lieutenant Commander?*"

"Yes. You earned it," Fuchida threw Hiryo a salute. "Now do a good job. Report to the Soryu. You'll join your squadron there."

Hiryo felt dazed as he returned the salute. *Imagine*, Hiryo thought. *Leading a carrier air group, a koku sentai! One of the elites!*

"It's a shame about Fuchida," Hiryo said to Lieutenant Sauto Harada, who sat next to him at dinner that night on the *Soryu*. "He led our attack against Pearl Harbor, and now he can't fly."

Harada, a member of Hiryo's squadron and proud of his role as Hiryo's wingman sighed, "And Genda, too. He's down with the flu."

"*Very* bad luck," Hiryo replied, shaking his head.

"No matter, sir. I'm confident we will win regardless."

They were interrupted as the ship's intercom crackled to life. "Attention! All hands! The Aleutian Islands have been invaded by our forces!"

A loud cheer went up in unison inside the dining room, followed by a hearty, *Banzai.*

Harada elbowed Hiryo. "See? How do you feel now?"

Hiryo nodded. "You're right. We will win." But something in his voice didn't sound entirely convinced.

Midway

In the early, balmy morning of June 4th, the Midway attack force of 36 Aichi D3A dive bombers and 36 Nakajima B5N torpedo bombers, escorted by 36 Mitsubishi A6M Zero fighters was assembled on the decks of the carriers.

Hiryo, in his brown pressed flying suit, sat in his Zero fighter preparing to lead the attack force.

The early morning dawn rose over the ocean to the east, painting streaks of yellow and red lines through the clouds, and Hiryo was given the order from the flight deck to commence take off.

He gunned the engine and roared down the flight deck of the Soryu amongst the cheers from the deck crew. As Fuchida had done before him at Pearl Harbor, Hiryo circled the fleet and waited for all planes to take their positions around him.

When done, Hiryo guided his fighter east and led his attack force toward Midway Island.

Thinking upon their victory at Pearl Harbor, Hiryo was in high spirits and confident they could accomplish the mission of neutralizing the enemy defenses at Midway.

An hour or so into their flight, they approached Midway Island, more of a rocky atoll than an island. Midway stood roughly equidistant between North America and Asia, thus the name, *Midway*.

Hiryo gave the order to attack, and the bombers broke away from the formation and proceeded to bomb the oil tanks on the island. The fighters dropped to the deck, strafing any and all planes that stood on the tarmac. Like Henderson Field at Pearl Harbor, Hiryo ripped through the rows of planes, scattering personnel and destroying everything he fired upon.

As he quickly rose into the sky for another pass at the ground installations, he could see the skies blacken from the burning oil tanks on the island that were spared at Pearl Harbor.

But this wasn't Pearl Harbor.

This time the enemy was prepared for the attack and their resistance was stiff. He saw two, then three of his bombers shot down by anti-aircraft fire that was both intense and deadly accurate.

Anti-aircraft fire erupted around him as well, buffeting his small plane. He heard a cry in his radio and looked over at his wingman, Harada. His Zero trailed white, then quickly turned to black fiery smoke from its underbelly as the plane quickly lost altitude, and Hiryo knew in an instant that Harada was a casualty.

The sound of bullets peppering his aircraft shook him from his thoughts as a U.S. Marine F4F fighter swooped down out of the glare of the sun.

It took all his skill of a fighter pilot to evade the American fighter, and using the advantage of the Zero, he turned inside of his attacker. He brought the enemy into sights of his guns and opened up on the pilot.

The Zero's 20mm cannon cut through the F4F shredding it to pieces. It exploded in the sky—*payment,* Hiryo thought, *for Harada's demise.*

Hiryo rose to 15,000 feet to survey the battle below him. Fuel was getting low, and he realized that the American resistance had blunted the attack. Though his bombers attacked Midway for over twenty minutes, and numerous enemy planes and hangars were destroyed, the airfield itself remained untouched.

Hiryo quickly radioed back to the fleet to update his status. "Enemy airfield still in tact. Enemy bombers are still able to refuel and attack our invasion force."

Indecision

"Sir," Fuchida said reporting to the bridge of the Akagi, "first strike force reports that a second strike is needed on Midway."

Before Nagumo could respond, a radio dispatch was thrust into his hands. Fuchida stood at attention, quietly waiting for Nagumo to review the report. Finally, after a few moments, Nagumo looked at Fuchida with a look of disbelief. "It's from Admiral Yamaguchi leading Carrier Division 2. He reports that an American carrier has been spotted northeast of Midway."

"That's impossible..." Fuchida replied. "It's supposed to be at Pearl Harbor."

"Well, it appears that it is *not!*" Nagumo snapped. "He also states that his carriers *Soryu* and *Hiryu,* along with ours, should immediately launch an attack on the American carrier."

"But what about our returning aircraft from Midway," Fuchida noted. "They are low on fuel. We must retrieve them as soon as they arrive or else risk them crashing into the sea."

There was a moment of uncertain silence on the bridge when someone yelled, "Enemy bomber!"

Fuchida and Nagumo looked up as an American B-26 bomber approached the *Akagi.* The bomber was trailed by smoke and flame and headed straight for their carrier, losing altitude fast. Worse, the American plane made no attempt to pull out of its plunge towards the *Akagi.*

"Hard to port!" Nagumo roared.

But fast maneuvers at this point would not be able to save the carrier. Fuchida and Nagumo watched on helplessly as the bomber barreled straight for the vessel, then at the last moment, it swerved out of control, narrowly missing the bridge and crashed into the sea.

Nagumo wasted no time in issuing his next orders. "Retrieve our planes. Re-arm them and launch our reserve for an attack on the American carrier. We will..."

"Enemy torpedo bombers!" screamed a lookout from the bridge. "Torpedo bombers to port!"

The bridge command gazed out over the water to see a dozen or more enemy torpedo bombers on both sides bearing down on the *Akagi*. Fuchida watched and could only assume it would be impossible to dodge all those torpedoes when launched.

But just as with the luck of the B-26 bomber, the gods of war smiled on Nagumo and the *Akagi*. The torpedo planes, without fighter escorts, were suddenly engaged by the protective cover of about fifty Zeros that quickly decimated their ranks and sent each one of the torpedo planes crashing into the sea.

The cheers and whistles that filled the carrier deck were short lived. More enemy torpedo planes appeared, roaring over the *Akagi* and made for the carrier *Hiryu*. They were successful in launching their torpedoes but the *Hiryu* managed to dodge each one.

Nagumo watched the attack with an incredulous expression. "That was over forty torpedo bombers. Far more than one American carrier could carry. There must be more American carriers nearby." He shot a look at Fuchida. "What are our scout planes saying?"

But Fuchida had no answer.

Without hesitation Nagumo replied, "The American carriers are the threat. Launch the attack with what we have on deck immediately. Inform Admiral Yamaguchi to do the same."

All their planes were in position and warming up as the *Akagi* turned into wind. Visibility was good with occasional breaks in the clouds above. Conversely, it gave good cover to any attacking planes above those very same clouds.

No sooner had the first Zero barreled down the flight deck and climbed into the sky when a lookout yelled, "Hell-divers!"

The bridge personnel looked up in the sky to see the menacing silhouettes of American *Dauntless* dive-bombers plummeting towards the ship. Three dark blue enemy planes quickly grew larger, and to Fuchida's growing horror, small black objects dropped from under their wings straight for the *Akagi*.

Fuchida dropped to the deck and scrambled behind some defensive sandbags on the bridge as the deafening sound of screaming bombs filled the air.

This was followed by the sound of one, two, then three massive explosions hitting the flight deck. The entire bridge personnel were knocked to the floor by the blasts.

There was a moment or two of eerie silence before a thundering explosion rolled towards them from the bowels of the ill-fated ship.

Fuchida stood up on unstable legs to see a huge, gaping hole in the flight deck near the stern elevator. The elevator itself was twisted like a pretzel and hung precariously into the hangar. Deck plates reeled upward in grotesque configurations and planes stood tail up, belching livid flame and jet-black smoke.

Planes, fuel tanks, bombs, and torpedoes quickly exploded, resulting in a holocaust of fire everywhere on deck.

Worse yet, the large carrier was beginning to list.

The *Akagi* was through. The great ship listed to port, and flames covered the once proud deck. The order was given to abandon ship.

Fuchida pleaded with Nagumo. "Sir, you must transfer your flag. Come, I'll assist you."

Fuchida made his way with Nagumo, and with the aide from other sailors, lowered themselves into lifeboats. As the boat pulled away, Fuchida gazed around him in horror.

Both the *Kaga* and the *Soryu* had suffered the same fate as the *Akagi*. All three ships were a mass of flame.

How could this have happened, Fuchida thought. *How?*

Inconceivable

Hiryo, his fighter badly damaged by machine gun fire and with a gaping hole in his wing that leaked fuel, dropped from out of the clouds to a frightening sight.

Not only was the *Soryu* carrier aflame from stem to stern, but the carriers *Kaga* and *Akagi* suffered a similar fate as well. Unable to land his stricken plane on the *Soryu*, he made for the *Hiryu* that had somehow escaped the carnage due to being further north and under heavy cloud cover.

Hiryo fought with the compromised controls of the Zero, desperately trying to keep the plane in the air. He pointed his fighter straight at the *Hiryu*, all the while praying he could keep it in the air long enough to touch down on its deck. As he reduced airspeed, the fighter started to swerve left then right and even begin to gain altitude. He struggled to keep the nose of the plane down and straight on course for the *Hiryu* that loomed larger and larger in his view.

Finally, as he approached the carrier, he dropped the nose and slammed hard into the wooden flight deck, skidding towards the elevator. He finally came to a jerking stop, shaken but relieved.

He was immediately surrounded by the deck crew, who helped him from the cockpit and then quickly pushed his wreck of a plane over the side before his fighter exploded.

"Are you all right, sir?" asked one of the crew.

Hiryo nodded his head. "I'm fine. But I need to report to the Flight Officer."

The crewmen directed him to the bridge, and Hiryo wasted no time in tracking the Flight Officer down.

"Our planes sunk an American carrier. We believe there are at least two more out there," the Flight Officer said. "You better get something to eat quickly because we will be mounting a counter attack very soon."

Hiryo had barely finished wolfing down his food when he heard over the ship's speaker, "All pilots, man your planes."

Hiryo rushed on deck and was directed by the same crewman to a new Zero that was prepared and ready for him. The crewman said nothing but gave Hiryo a look that he fully understood.

Revenge.

Hiryo climbed into his fighter, fired up the engine and waited for the signal to take off.

Given, the wheels of his Zero left the flight deck, and he rose to join up with the small attack force bent on finding the American carriers.

Once their planes darkened the skies; now just a handful of fighters, torpedo planes and bombers would decide if the Japanese could snatch victory from the jaws of defeat.

He was only several hundred feet from the *Hiryu* when he looked back in horror. The ship was under attack by dive-bombers.

The *Hiryu* was hit once, twice and a third time by armor piercing bombs. The stricken carrier erupted in flames that quickly engulfed the entire flight deck. The stricken carrier was at a point of maximum vulnerability when a fresh assault of bombs were dropped onto the massed planes preparing to take off. The fully gassed and bomb filled planes began to detonate one by one, setting off a chain reaction of explosions.

Now all four carriers, the very pride of the Imperial Navy, had been crippled by bombs and were burning uncontrollably.

Hiryo steeled himself against the scene. Even though he would have no place to land when he returned, there was still a mission to complete. Still an American carrier to destroy.

Leaving the chaos of the fleet behind, he joined the small attack force in search of the American carriers.

Marginalized

Approximately one hour later, the second attack wave of ten torpedo bombers and six escorting Zeros arrived over an enemy carrier under steam and unleashed a ferocious attack.

Hiryo's Zero and five other escort fighters strafed the deck of the carrier, thereby suppressing the ship's anti-aircraft fire. One after another, they drove 20mm cannon fire into the carrier's steel hull.

As the escort Zeros pulled up, the torpedo bombers launched their attack, skimming the ocean and releasing torpedoes. Each torpedo hit its mark as the carrier exploded into flames. Fires belched from deep below its deck and erupted through the elevators in an all-consuming maelstrom of searing heat.

With the successful assault accomplished, Hiryo turned his Zero around and flew in wide circles hoping to locate the fleet.

He eyed his fuel gauge where it hovered just above empty, and the sea below him looked as empty as his fuel. But then he saw a ship dotted on the horizon. It was a cruiser leaving a wide wake.

If he could reach that wake...

His engine abruptly and went silent. Time was up.

With the propeller feathered in the wind, Hiryo guided his aircraft towards the wake. He knew he had only one chance of a fairly soft landing.

The belly of his Zero slowly eased itself into the wide wake, skimming the water's surface and Hiryo touched the nose down to a bumpy landing. But his moment to savor his good fortune was short-lived as the Zero quickly filled with ocean water. Hiryo quickly unstrapped his harness, scrabbled from the cockpit and pulled himself into the water.

As he bobbed along the surface of the water, he watched with growing hope and desperation, as the cruiser loomed closer. Then, when the ship approached within one hundred yards, several American B-17s materialized overhead and the cruiser quickly changed course and sped off in the opposite direction.

Hiryo watched helplessly as the ship grew smaller, leaving him alone in the water and his best hope for survival evaporating like mist in the wind.

The sun started to set, the ocean reflected a dusky hue, and soon darkness consumed him. He drifted in the water for hours and Hiryo prepared himself for certain death.

As consciousness began to slip, he saw a distant light flashing a dim recognition code. It was Japanese. Adrenaline kicked in and Hiryo thrashed around in the sea in the hopes that the white water and bioluminescence would attract the ship. After several minutes of this effort, the action proved successful. A Japanese destroyer navigated towards him and lowered a lifeboat that made its way towards Hiryo.

Several minutes later, he was pulled aboard, but once again, his elation quickly turned to revulsion.

As he gazed around him, his eyes were filled with men missing hands and legs, faces and bodies disfigured and burned beyond recognition. Many cried out, "Kurushii, kurushii!" The mangled sailors were begging for water and some called out to their mothers.

As Hiryo stood transfixed in a daze, a doctor looked up from treating a sailor with a severed leg. "Do you need to be treated?"

Hiryo refocused and waved him off. "I'm fine. Treat the others."

Then the doctor replied with bitter finality. "No. I *will* treat you. You can still fly and engage the enemy. These men," as he pointed to the suffering humanity around him, "are useless for the purpose of fighting."

And that was a realization for Hiryo that hit home and shattered the final myth of the glories of battle. For soldiers were stripped of their humanity in combat. They were seen not as individual persons, but mere cogs of war; commodities to be used only as weapons of destruction. If you were not severely injured, you were simply patched up and returned to the fight. If you were severely injured, you were marginalized; just another non-functional weapons; useless.

Incognito

Under strict orders, Hiryo reported to sickbay to be treated. As he walked in he saw, sitting in a corner waiting for attention, none other than *Harada*. His arm was in a sling, but otherwise he looked no worse for wear.

Hiryo stood dumbfounded for a moment before gaining his wits and rushing to Harada's side. "You're alive! I swear I thought... well you know..."

"You're not the only good pilot in this navy," he joked.

"So, I guess you'll be sent home to recover. Have you written your family yet to let them know you're alive?"

Harada shook his head. "Orders. We're not allowed to write or receive letters until further notice. And you yourself will be confined to base for at least a month."

"But why?"

"Because of our poor performance at Midway," Harada uttered. "The government doesn't want the news of our loss to get out too soon. At least, give them time to put the proper spin on it and create a victory instead," he said bitterly. "The truth would only demoralize our people and the troops."

Hiryo felt a surge of anger replace the excitement in seeing his comrade. "But we lost good men in the fight, not to mention four of our first line carriers. They deserve better than to be political lies."

Harada nodded. "The realities of war, my friend," Hiryo sighed. "And what will they do with you and the other wounded?"

"Rumor has it that we will be transferred to naval hospitals and classified as *secret* patients. We will be placed in isolation wards and quarantined from other patients to keep this major defeat nothing more than an ugly secret."

Harada reached out his hand and placed it on Hiryo's shoulder. "Be careful, my friend. There are other rumors as well. They say that the officers and men that survived the battle will be dispersed to other units far from Japan." He shrugged and let out a strained laugh. "And as for me, being a *secret* patient in a navy hospital is not all bad. At least the food will be good."

Rabaul

As I reeled in and out of consciousness, I knew not where I was, nor what time or day it was. I stared up into the fiery sun from the undulating lifeboat that held me captive on an almost calm sea. Nakatomi had succumbed to his wounds and I covered him with a tattered tarp. I wanted his body, and mine as well, to be found for our family's sake.

The blistering days ran into shivering nights and the nights into days. In addition to the lack of food, the burning near equatorial sun had slowly dehydrated me from lack of water and added to my bouts of semi-consciousness.

In between rounds of delusion and lucidity, I would imagine ships on the horizon making their way to rescue me from my bitter fate. At night I would dream myself back to my family in America, filled with regret in having deserted them in search of a Japan that no longer existed. Worst of all, I would never be able to say my proper goodbyes.

In one period of nightly lucidness, huddled under the canopy of the lifeboat, with waves relentlessly slapping against the sides, the ghostly veil covering my awareness was sharply pulled away.

It was the sound of a horn. *A ship's horn.*

I pulled myself up and scanned the ocean's mirrored surface, squinting through inflamed eyes.

And although the image stood blurred and twisted before me, it was a ship. A vessel heading straight towards me.

I reached out with my good arm as if to touch the specter coming my way when the horn blared again. This time even louder. The ship was coming closer and a thought crossed my mind.

I wish it were an American ship. A ship that would take me away from this god-forsaken war.

I slipped back into semi-consciousness, giving myself up to whatever fate awaited me, when I felt strong limbs lift me from the lifeboat.

"He's coming to, Doctor," I heard a voice stated.

I tried to focus on the voice's location and saw white clean walls. Bright light. And I could feel the clean starched sheets that covered me. I was surprised to find that both my hands were functional, though my left arm was bound to prevent movement.

My attention turned to a young Japanese corpsman standing over me.

"Where am I?" my haggard voice croaked.

"Be still," a second man coaxed. He wore a white coat with the rank of major adorned on his shoulders. "You have suffered from severe exposure and a trauma to your left arm. I'm Doctor Miyakazi and you are in a naval hospital in Rabaul."

"Rabaul?"

"Hai. In Papua New Guinea."

That made little sense to me since I had only a vague idea of where New Guinea was located.

Miyakazi picked up my bandaged arm and slowly removed the gauze wrapping. "Healing nicely." As he reapplied fresh gauze, he turned his eyes on mine. "Now. What is your name and who was the man with you in the lifeboat? His clothing and identification were too burned to read. And your ID was unreadable from the salt water. How long have you been adrift in the lifeboat?"

I managed to tell him the story of the sinking of the *Shoho* and how I found a lifeboat adrift with Nakatomi inside it. "Nakatomi's next of kin should be notified, and I need to contact my editor as soon as possible. I bet he gave me up for lost."

Miyakazi nodded. "Of course. You rest for now. We'll contact your newspaper and Nakatomi's family."

As I started to doze off, all I could think was that I was still trapped in this ugly war. Then a thought crossed my mind. I wondered if Sakura was going to dock me three weeks pay.

Knowing him, he probably would.

Reproachment

"Ultimately, we had very bad luck," Nagumo stated dryly as he stood before a long, wooden table, addressing all the powers-that-be of the Naval General Staff.

Yamamoto banged on the table. "Bad luck?!" His eyes twisted in equal part rage and discomfort due to the stomach cramps he had come down with on his way back from Midway. "You broke a standing order of not committing your reserve force!"

"We had no other choice," Nagumo countered. "American carriers had appeared, and that was the overriding threat. We were forced to use what we had at the time to counter the attack."

"And what of your fighter air cover? You lost control," Yamamoto snapped. "They took off in chase of the first American torpedo bombers instead of regaining altitude to protect our carriers. Through your blatant recklessness, we lost four carriers to the Americans' one. *Four!*"

Yamamoto struggled to stay composed. "We lost the very best of our pilots and their aircrews, *and* their experience. Losses we will be hard pressed to replace."

The direness of Yamamoto's voice quieted the room. Even Nagumo knew the consequences of Midway—they might just have lost the war.

"I must apologize to His Majesty for my failure," Nagumo said.

Yamamoto abruptly stood up. "No. I will be the one to apologize to His Majesty. It was my plan that lead to this defeat."

"Commander," an aide dressed in a crisp Imperial Marine uniform announced at Fujiyama's office door. "There's someone here that wants to speak with you."

Fujiyama barely looked up from a thick stack of paperwork. "Not now. I'm very busy preparing a report for the Admiral."

"But he says it's important," the Marine replied. "And wants to speak only to you."

Fujiyama stared at the Marine.

"He says he is a friend of Kenta Hiyakawa, and he has a message for you."

Fujiyama stiffened at hearing Hiyakawa's name.

"Send him in."

The Marine nodded and quickly escorted a thin Japanese man who was properly dressed in a pin-stripped suit, red tie, and white shirt into the room.

The thin man bowed to Fujiyama and said in a low voice, "Excuse me for the interruption. My name is Toshikazu Kase. I'm told that you are a friend of Kenta Hiyakawa."

"Yes. Do you have message from him or about his wife?"

"No." He paused for a moment, looking unsure of himself. "Is it safe to speak here? What I have to say is very confidential."

Fujiyama stood and closed his office door. "How do you know Hiyakawa?"

"We served together for a brief time in the diplomatic corps. Before the war."

"So what do you want to tell me?" Fujiyama was getting anxious with the man's ambiguous nature and wanted to finish the report for Yamamoto.

"The British Ambassador, Sir Robert Craigie and I, became good friends. After he was interned when the war began, I visited him secretly on several occasions."

Fujiyama reached for the door handle, prepared to end the

impromptu meeting. "That's very nice of you for taking such a risk for a friend but..."

"Please, sir. Hear me out," Kase implored.

Fujiyama sighed. "Fine. But please get to your point."

"Just before the war, I was entrusted by Foreign Minister Togo with a highly confidential message for the British Embassy. I was surprised at what I was told to relay to Sir Robert." Kase then spoke very concisely, "The message regarded the eventual restoration of peace."

"Go on," Fujiyama said. "I'm listening."

Kase cleared his throat and continued. "The message was simple. *Should it happen that the British Government became desirous of discussing or negotiating peace they would find the Japanese Government ready to be helpful.*"

"And what did the ambassador say?"

"He led me to believe that this would be possible."

Fujiyama tried to mask his shock. But this little man seemed credible enough. If there was any truth to it, this information should be pursued as it might prove to be a way to end the war with honor.

"I'm telling you this since you are a friend of Hiyakawa's, and a like soul with the same feelings as others about the war. I seriously doubt the politicians would pursue this, but if someone in the military with close ties to the Emperor could raise the subject..."

Fujiyama knew what he meant. *Inform Yamamoto.*

"But what about Foreign Minister Togo? Why not have him talk to the Emperor?" Fujiyama knew it was a stupid question as soon as he voiced the words. The military was in charge now, not the politicians.

Kase didn't bother answering Fujiyama's query. "I leave this information with you, sir," Kase said instead. "Please do what you can."

After the man took his leave, Fujiyama immediately picked up his phone and dialed Yamamoto's office.

New Plans

Yamamoto seated himself across the table filled with members of the Diet in the Emperor's Palace. Prince Chichibu was also in attendance, which Yamamoto considered rather odd.

As he gave his Midway Operation report, he was prepared to take full responsibility and ready to face any consequences the Emperor deemed fit.

At the conclusion of the report, the Emperor just sat there, unreadable. After a few moments of dull silence, he only asked a single question. "Does the nation know of our defeat?"

"Only the Aleutian Operation," Yamamoto replied. "The capture of two small islands in the chain, Attu and Kiska, were mentioned in the newspapers. Nothing was said of the Midway encounter itself, and all references to Midway were deleted from official reports. The only people who know the true extent of the defeat are the Naval General Staff."

The Emperor remained quiet for some time, and all in the room waited nervously for him to speak. "Is there anything else?"

"Hai," replied Yamamoto. He had mulled over what Fujiyama had told him about Kase's visit and informed the Emperor of everything, even in the presence of Prince Chichibu.

"If this is true, Your Majesty, we could pursue peace and retain the Empire we have acquired," Yamamoto stated.

A murmuring of dissent circulated around the table, but Yamamoto kept his attention on Prince Chichibu's reaction.

The man's body language was not good, yet he said nothing.

"What are your plans from here?" the Emperor asked as if he had not heard a single word Yamamoto had just said.

Realizing that interest in pursuing peace was not on the table, Yamamoto replied, "We have planned to extend our Empire south, from New Guinea, with the objective of establishing bases to support possible future advances in order to seize Fiji and Samoa. This effort will sever the supply lines between Australia and the United States with the goal of eliminating Australia as a threat to us in the South Pacific."

Prince Chichibu finally spoke a single word: "When?"

"We have secured Rabaul in February and are capturing the Solomon Islands, which was the first step towards invading Fiji and Samoa. This has already begun with occupation of Guadalcanal on June 9th. I will move my headquarters to Rabaul to oversee the campaign."

The Emperor nodded. "And does the Naval General Command agree with your plans?

"Yes, Your Majesty."

"Let us hope that this plan works better for us than Midway."

With that, the Emperor rose, signaling an end of the meeting.

Truth

As the summer came to a gradual close, and the weather started to cool, the prison political atmosphere changed as well, but for the worse for Connor and Barbara, who were looked upon as some kind of subversive element and treated accordingly.

But it wasn't *all bad* for Connor.

He and Barbara had long conversations about Japan, and she slowly honed Connor's Japanese to where he spoke almost as effortlessly as a native. One day, as they took their daily permitted walk, he asked Barbara how she knew so much about the Japanese and their culture.

"I studied Asian culture in college, focusing my studies on Japan." She smiled as she reflected back upon her youth. "That's where I met Mr. Hiyakawa. I was young and became immediately smitten with his gentle manner and polite charm. He was a rising star in the diplomatic corps, and I learned so much from him about Japan. The good and the not so good."

She sighed, then her smile brightened even more. "It wasn't long until we were married, and I never regretted one moment of it."

"Did your parents object to marrying outside your race?"

"Oh, yes. Very much so," she said, nodding her head. "And when he was recalled to Japan in 1930, I went with him, of course. I didn't realize it at the time, but my loyalty to my husband pretty much severed ties with my own family."

"So, in a way," Connor noted, "you're an outcast like me?"

"Yes, perhaps I am." She took his hand in hers. "Come, it's time to get back to our cells."

When they returned to their quarters, Little Glass Eye stood waiting for them. And he was smiling.

"What do you want?" Barbara asked defiantly.

The smile quickly disappeared from Little Glass Eye's lips as he growled, "Watch yourself, American whore." He resisted the urge to beat her for arrogance because after several months of constant punishment—mental and physical—Barbara had adapted herself to the humiliation, and the guards could see the punishment no longer had the effect on her psyche that they wished for.

"I want to introduce you to someone," Little Glass Eye said.

From behind him, footsteps were heard shuffling down the hall toward their cell. A tall American POW, who might have been stocky and burley at one time but was now gaunt from battle, appeared at their cell door. The man wore another distinction as well. Part of his cheek was gone; only a sunken hole of tattered flesh remained. Perhaps from a bullet wound to the face.

Below that hideous wound, a last name had been stitched on his ragged tan uniform. *Williams.*

The recognition of the man and Connor was both immediate and mutual.

"Connor," the American soldier said with a nasty grin that only made the hole in his cheek even more vile. "So you made it here to your people. What happened? Did that nip nanny of yours bring you here?"

Connor's face drained of color, and an expression of utter detest ravaged his young face.

"Now, is that any way to greet your father," Williams laughed.

"Get out of here," Connor demanded.

Little Glass Eye appeared delighted and amused at this unexpected turn of events. "He's not going anywhere, boy," Little Glass Eye smirked. "In fact, he is the custodian of this cell block."

"A POW?" Barbara practically shouted.

"New rules," Little Glass Eye replied. "We use those that are willing to cooperate with us." He paused a moment and grinned. "After all, wouldn't you want some of your own kind overseeing you? I'll leave you all to get better acquainted."

After Little Glass Eye departed the cell, Connor glared at the man who was his biological father. "How did you get here? I thought you were in America."

"Had to take my leave," Williams replied with a sardonic smile. "Although it was an unfortunate accident, it seems the law thought I had something to do with the death of your mother. So I joined the Army. Regrettably for me, the U.S. went to war." His hand inadvertently reached up for the disfigurement on his face.

"It was no accident," Connor spit. "You beat her constantly when I was a child."

"So what are you going to do?" Williams laughed. "Arrest me?"

Connor's eyes glazed over from years of frustration and anger, and he threw himself at Williams who easily grabbed his son by the arm and slammed him onto the concrete floor.

"Stop it!" yelled Barbara. "He's just a boy!"

"He's more than that," Williams growled.

Puzzled by his response, Barbara then remembered the curious statement he made just a few short moments ago. "You said he made it here to his people. What do you mean by that?"

Williams scowled. "He's a dirty Jap is what I meant."

Connor sat upon the floor and grabbed at his head. "Jap...?"

"Are you really that thick? You're half Japanese, half Ainu, and I never forgave your mother for lying to me before we got married." He grabbed Connor by the top of his shirt and towered over the boy. "That's why I beat her. She broke the law. She deserved what she got."

He dropped Connor back to the floor. Hatred and disgust filled his eyes.

"What's the matter, Connor? Didn't Fujiyama tell you? Didn't he tell you that you're half-Jap?"

Connor was speechless. *Why didn't Meiko tell him? Why didn't Fujiyama?*

"Now you have to live with it, just like I have." Williams gave Barbara a lurid stare and stormed out of the cell.

"I don't understand," Connor sobbed. "How...? Why...? He can't be right? My mother had blonde hair and blue eyes just like me."

Perched on the bunk along side of him, Barbara clutched his hand and whispered softly. "He said she was Ainu, native Japanese islanders from Hokkaido. They can look very European. They have fair skin and many have light colored hair and blue eyes." She squeezed his hand tighter. "If your mother didn't reveal she was Japanese before marrying your father, then she broke the law. The law against miscegenation, a mixed race law against marriage."

Connor wiped the tears from his eyes that wouldn't abate. "But why did he have to beat her to death? He loved her at one time..."

"Your father, for whatever reason, hates the Japanese and thinks them to be sub-human. Unfortunately, he's like many Americans today."

Connor was quiet for some time, just staring at the floor.

Then he raised his head and stared into Barbara's kind eyes. "I can look on the bright side. That means I'm no longer an ijin. I'm Japanese."

Guadalcanal

"How does it feel to be re-joining your old unit?" asked Major Okada as the troop ship they stood upon plowed through the dark South Pacific night.

"How does it feel to be promoted from Captain to *Major*?" Yoshi replied.

Okada smiled. "Hai. I didn't want it, but the war being what it is..." He stared out at the rolling sea from the railing of the troop transport, navigating what was known in the Guadalcanal Campaign as *The Slot*. "We're not doing that well on Guadalcanal. The Americans control the only airfield on the island, and the U.S. Marines are becoming quite a group of Samurais."

Yoshi gazed out over the dark waters as well. "Will you be commanding our unit again, now that you've been promoted?"

"Yes. But as a Division Commander in charge of several Companies like yours."

Yoshi thought for a moment then waved his hand over the ocean and the convoy of ships. "Sir. Do you think with these many re-enforcements we could push the Americans off the island?"

Major Okada patted Yoshi on the shoulder. "We will try. That's all I know."

They stood in silence for a few minutes until Yoshi asked a nagging question. "Private Taka. Did he survive the Philippine battles?"

"Hai. He made it out of the Corregidor Invasion in one piece.

You'll see him soon. He's on Guadalcanal with the rest of your unit. He's..."

The sound of aircraft engines overhead silenced both men.

"Ours or theirs?" Yoshi asked.

Okada listened for another moment before replying. "Ours. Bombers by the sound of the engines. On their way to bomb the American airfield." He rubbed at his clean-shaven jaw and lowered his voice. "Between our ships being bombed by their planes, attacked by their warships, or shelled from Guadalcanal, it's a wonder we can land re-enforcements at all. Why our fleet hasn't neutralized their naval and air elements I don't honestly understand. What are they waiting for?"

Okada then abruptly changed the subject. "We will be disembarking in a few hours. You better go down to the mess hall and eat. If we face resistance, you may not be eating for a while."

As the sun rose over the palm trees on the cove the next morning, Yoshi found himself on a 2,500 square-mile section of an island covered by dense jungle and high, looming hills. Guadalcanal stood dominated by the Kavo Mountains, which reach up to 8,000 feet. Rains pound the island almost every day, and the nights turn chilly, forcing men in ill-suited clothing to huddle together for warmth.

Because of the incessant harassment from the Americans down The Slot, most of the oil drums of supplies that made it to the island had to be towed behind submarines at night, with buoys attached to mark them, and left offshore. Soldiers hid in the jungle and had to retrieve them before the sun rose, but many of them were so weak from malnutrition that they couldn't retrieve the oil drums.

Yoshi found himself immediately put to work, helping to unload the drums of food for the troops stationed on the island.

It was hot in the cove as well, and the humid air stuck to his skin like a second set of clothing. Another irritation also found a home on his skin. *Mosquitoes.* Hordes of them had appeared out of the jungle, and several of the voracious insects had decided to use Yoshi as their dining pleasure. He was constantly swatting at the pests as he unpacked the oil drums of rice, powdered miso and soy sauce, matches, candles, and other vital items.

Yoshi looked up from his work and grimaced. A solemn procession of Japanese soldiers stumbled out of the jungle and into the cove. The group of young men barely appeared human. They were skin and bones, dressed in ragged military uniforms, and looked more like sticks of bamboo than men.

"A sad sight," Okada said as he stepped up to Yoshi. "Our troops are surviving on will alone." He shook his head, then touched Yoshi on the arm. "Come. I have something else for you to do."

Okada led the young soldier to the end of the cove where several dozen, small wooden boxes had been arranged on the beach. And next to the boxes were various piles of human bones, some white and others the color of coal.

"The white ones are the remains of our honored dead that were cremated," Okada said somberly. "For those soldiers, there was time for proper cremation." He then pointed to the piles of fragmented bones that were charred and blackened. "And those are the remains of soldiers at the front. Unfortunately, there was not sufficient time to cremate them properly."

Seeing this travesty, Yoshi's blood boiled with anger. What horrible creed had given the orders in this war that such men should end life in this way?

Okada noticed Yoshi's mood. "I know this is not a pleasant task, but the remains of these men should be sent home to their families. It's the least we can do. So please place the remains and any personal items with them in the small boxes."

Yoshi nodded and began the solemn task.

Camp

The next day, Yoshi joined his unit camping in a small ravine. Some of the young men that he had trained with in boot camp were there. Although worn and tired, these soldiers looked in much better condition than the specters he witnessed in the cove the previous day.

But many of the new recruits were untested in battle, having never fired a shot. He couldn't help but wonder how they would react when finally forced to take action. Like most, once the shooting started, he feared that they would take cover, hug the earth, and simply pray for mercy.

When the group of untested soldiers saw Yoshi, sporting his Corporal stripes, some of them rushed up to congratulate him.

"So, you're the boss of our squad," a small soldier with a shaved head asked.

Yoshi recognized the young man from the battle at Bataan. "Hai." Then with false bravado, "And you better obey my orders."

The men laughed and slapped Yoshi on the back in a sign of comradeship. But Yoshi's light mood instantly shifted when Taka rushed up to him and tried to give him a hug.

"Back off, Taka," Yoshi spat.

Taka stiffened. "Pulling rank on your old war comrade?"

"You're no comrade of mine, Taka. Just obey my orders, *Private,* and keep your distance from me."

"Enough talk," roared Sergeant Gunso as he came up on the

group of soldiers. Though Gunso had not lost any of his usual bluster, Yoshi found himself glad to see the professional warrior.

"We're moving out. Corporal, get your squad together." Yoshi nodded and ordered his squad to join the long line of troops heading into the jungle.

In a few short hours, the company of men had entered a coconut grove with tall amber grass that grew up to their chest. Yoshi was leading his squad when his foot stumbled upon something lying on the ground. He looked down to see a body sprawled in the grass. It was a lowly dead Japanese private with his backpack at his side and his head resting on his boots in which he stored his emergency rice.

The private may have been hidden in the tall grass for a while, but in the brutal climate of the jungle, the soldier could have been there for just a short amount of time. The boy's face was already badly decomposed and maggots tumbled from his mouth and nose.

Yoshi kneeled and said a short prayer over the young private when Gunso snapped. "Keep moving, Corporal. There's nothing you can do for him now."

The tall grass soon gave way to nearly impenetrable, stifling jungle, and after an agonizing torment of plodding through the narrow paths overshadowed by high trees and canopies of screeching birds, the company rested for a meager lunch while nestled in a small ravine.

Taka took a seat beside Yoshi and sipped on some miso soup from his mess tin. "I think we're going to try and take the American airfield again. We took this way the last time we attacked." Trying to get a laugh out of Yoshi, he remarked, "I think I recognize that tree."

Yoshi was not amused but stopped picking the weevils out of his rice and asked, "You were on the last attack?"

"Hai," Taka replied conceitedly. "Before you arrived."

Seeing that Yoshi was a little more amiable towards him, Taka ventured into some small talk. "Do you know the three items most important for survival in the jungle?"

Yoshi feigned disinterest.

Taka sat up erect like he was about to give a lecture. "Well, they are salt, matches, and a mess tin to cook rice in. You need salt in this stiffing heat. Without it, you will be unable to walk. You can't keep cooked rice because it will cake."

"I know that," Yoshi snapped. "You have to eat it right after you cook it."

Taka nodded fervently. "And the mess tin is light and compact to cook the rice. Even boots are not a necessity. If they wear out, just take better ones from a dead soldier." Taka took on a more serious voice, "Death awaits soldiers who lacked those three items."

Yoshi, unimpressed with the lecture just nodded and went back to eating his paltry rations.

Footsteps came up from behind them, and Major Okada, who clutched a Type 97 Anti-Tank rifle, stared down at Yoshi. "Corporal Fujiyama, I want you and another soldier to use this in our assault tomorrow."

Yoshi had seen the Type 97 in basic training. It was a beast of a weapon. To call it a rifle was a serious understatement. The weapon used a mammoth round and was extremely unwieldy to tote around, thus the need for two men. But these drawbacks did not hamper its success against the American Sherman tanks.

"Take him," Okada ordered, pointing to Taka. "He is trained on how to use it properly."

Though Yoshi was not happy having to depend of Taka, he nodded. "Yes, Sir."

Soon, a violent clasp of thunder erupted around them, followed by a light drizzle. A gentle breeze swept in, and it felt good against the sticky humid air of the island.

It was going to be a wet night.

That evening Yoshi fell into a restless sleep but was awakened at four in the morning by a vicious downpour of rain that rustled through the jungle canopy above. Yoshi covered his head and crouched under the sparse protection of the leaves of a banana plant. The smell of fresh rain and ocean air permeated his senses, but exhaustion prevailed and he eventually fell back into a troubled sleep.

Coward

The next morning, despite the hot sun returning with an unrelenting vengeance, the unit found itself formed and ready to assault the airfield the Americans called Henderson Field. After days of pounding rain, the soldier's uniforms remained damp and smelled of mold.

Then there was the diarrhea epidemic. Sleeping on the wet ground at night cooled their stomachs and caused every soldier to suffer chronic bouts of the dreaded condition.

Yoshi had not been immune to any of this. In addition, he hadn't been able to properly wash his body or face, nor brush his teeth for nearly a month. As a result, one of his upper front teeth had chipped off, and his entire body smelled like a wild dog.

In the near distance, the troops could see Marine fighters and Navy Douglas bombers rising in the air from the airfield on their way to attack the Japanese.

"Let's hope they don't spot us in this thick jungle," Okada said as he knelt beside Yoshi and Taka, their anti-tank rifle situated between them.

Suddenly, bullets from a machine gun whizzed past Yoshi's helmet and were quickly followed by artillery rounds falling just behind them.

Yoshi threw himself face down and pressed his body into the jungle carpet of wet leaves and moss. The air around them quickly filled with the pungent smell of gunpowder and the sharp tang of cordite as the artillery shells exploded closer and closer to the unit.

"Get up!" Okada ordered as the artillery rounds ripped through the trees overhead. He drew his long *Shin Gunso* military service sword and bellowed over the chaos, "Keep moving! Keep moving!"

Yoshi struggled to his feet but quickly stumbled into a crater of freshly cut soil. From his hands and knees, he stared in horror at the sight. The bomb crater was not only filled with rainwater, but something else as well. Wounded men who were unable to pull themselves out of the waterlogged pit, floated facedown in the brown and red-tinged water.

Yoshi pressed his eyes closed and scrambled through the watery grave as the barrage of artillery fire continued. Thickets of bush and bamboo trees were blown to shreds, sending large clumps of dirt and shards of wood through the air like missiles.

A 60mm mortar round exploded behind him, tossing Yoshi forward and into a shell crater.

Ears ringing and with blurred vision, Yoshi slowly got his wits about him only to see an American Marine standing over him at the rim of the crater. The Marine had his bayonet pointed at Yoshi's chest and was preparing to use it.

I'm dead, Yoshi thought. He closed his eyes, prayed silently, and waited for the inevitable.

A spine-chilling scream filled the air, and Yoshi felt an object rip past him. He opened his eyes and spotted the Marine's severed head resting next to his. Standing in the very spot where the Marine had stood, he saw Okada gripping his long service sword and the blade running with fresh blood.

"Your backpack is burning!" Okada cried. "Take it off!"

In all the chaos, Yoshi hadn't felt the burning pack strapped to his back until Okada yelled at him. He quickly yanked off the smoldering pack and dropped it to the ground.

"Are you hurt?" Okada asked as he pulled Yoshi from the pit.

Yoshi took inventory of his body. No pain. Limbs intact. He shook his head.

"Find Taka and let's move," Okada ordered.

Yoshi raced upon the scorched earth and found Taka huddled in a shell crater with the Type 97 Anti-Tank rifle pressed to his chest.

The barrage of gunfire abruptly ceased, only to be replaced by the rumble and roar of a massive engine. Moments later, an M-4 Sherman tank crested the hill in front of them and headed in their direction.

Okada raised his sword and screamed at Yoshi and Taka. "Bring that 97 up!"

Yoshi's first impulse was to run in the opposite direction, but his mind overpowered the urge. *Honor*, he kept saying to himself. *Honor and courage*.

Yoshi helped Taka lug the anti-tank rifle, but they made slow progress through the wet mud and grass. So much so that Okada and a squad of infantry had already advanced well ahead of them up the hill. They were trying to outflank the rumbling tank in order to give Taka a good shot.

Okada looked back over his shoulder from his prone position. "Move up! Take your shot!"

"Let's go!" Yoshi yelled at Taka, but the young man froze in terror. "What the hell. *Taka?!*"

Then Yoshi's worst fears of Taka were quickly realized. Eyes filled with paralyzing fear, Taka threw the anti-tank rifle on the ground and fled in the opposite direction.

"*Damn it, Taka!*" Yoshi screamed. He turned and watched helplessly as the Sherman's machine gun sprayed the area where Okada and his men were positioned.

As the machine gun peppered the dirt field around his comrades, Yoshi could see rows of machine gun fire raking the soldiers in front of him like sitting ducks.

Yoshi grabbed the anti-tank rifle and lugged it forward. Hugging the ground as the best he could, Yoshi moved towards Okada. Screams of wounded men filled his ears, pleading for help, but Yoshi pressed on. When he reached the major, Yoshi saw that he was riddled with bullets. "I'll get you out of here, sir."

"The tank!" Okada screamed. "Get the tank before it kills us all."

Yoshi looked up to see the Sherman turn towards the remaining troops on the field, continuing to fire its 75mm cannon, belching smoke and fire.

Yoshi lifted the heavy weapon onto his shoulder, took aim and fired. The recoil ripped into his shoulder and tossed Yoshi to the ground as the armor-piercing round struck the tank mid-center. A small fiery hole erupted into a blast so large it blew the turret clear off the lumbering tank and Yoshi felt a blanket of heat against his face.

Okada's bloodied hand reached up and grabbed Yoshi's arm. "Good job, soldier." Then with a gasp, he slumped to the broken ground.

"Sir?" Yoshi said, as he shook his commander. "Sir!" Sorrow quickly turned to resignation, and resignation turned to hatred. Hatred towards the Imperial Operations Staff. Hatred for the cowardly Taka. Yoshi slipped Okada's service pistol from its holster and went in search of the coward responsible.

Yoshi's search didn't take long. He found Taka running from the field back towards the jungle. "Enough, Taka!" Yoshi commanded, but the young man looked back over his shoulder with wide terrified eyes and kept fleeing.

Taka was almost to the jungle when out of the dense foliage came another Sherman tank. Taka didn't spot the enemy and tripped over a vine.

Sprawled on his back, he watched the steel beast rumble towards him. Taka rolled to the side to avoid being crushed by the monster but was caught in the Sherman's massive treads.

The drive sprocket of the tank's treads picked up Taka's body and swallowed him as easily as a clump of dirt. Screams were cut short as he went around the tread twice, and what was left of his tattered body sloughed off onto the jungle floor, unrecognizable as a human being.

The Sherman then turned its turret towards Yoshi and fired its machine gun. Yoshi hugged the muddy ground, trying to compress himself into the earth.

The 75mm gun of the Sherman roared and a shell exploded just yards from Yoshi's body. The concussion felt like a sharp punch to the stomach, and his eardrums pulsated as a wave of nausea consumed him.

Another loud explosion followed as an aircraft roared over Yoshi's head. He stared up from the ground and watched a Zero fly over him, leaving the Sherman engulfed in flames behind it.

Yoshi stood but found his legs were like rubber. He struggled to keep his balance, and his head swam from the near miss of the Sherman's shell.

And he was exhausted.

Both physically and mentally.

He was angry and disgusted. Depending on hand-to-hand combat and Banzai charges was madness when the enemy had such highly developed weapons.

But he did his duty, with both honor and courage—not for the Emperor that he had sworn to serve, but on behalf of himself.

Bad News

After fully recovering from my weeks adrift in the ocean, I learned from the hospital staff that Rabaul was Yamamoto's headquarters in the South Pacific. That meant there was a good chance Fujiyama would be here as well.

As I was being discharged from the hospital, I pulled aside the head doctor and asked, "How can I get message to Yamamoto's headquarters?"

The doctor, an affable Naval Commander, was perfectly blunt. "I don't know your chances of seeing Admiral Yamamoto. From what I understand, he's quite busy these days."

"It's not him I want to contact," I replied, packing the last of the personal items supplied to me by the hospital. "I have good friend on his staff that I'd like to see. *If he's there.*"

"Well, let's find out," the doctor replied. We walked to the administration building and entered the Commander's office. He instructed his aide, a young seaman, to connect us to Yamamoto's headquarters. "Who do you want to speak to?"

"Commander Akihito Fujiyama. He's supposed to be on Yamamoto's staff," I replied. "Tell him Yoshihara Koga is on Rabaul and wants to see him."

A few minutes later, we heard the aide mumble over the phone, "Hai. Good. Please give him the message." He hung up and reported his conversation. "There is a Commander Fujiyama there at headquarters, but he was not available. I left a message for you."

"Domo," I replied. "If he returns the call, I'll be in the hospital cafeteria."

✷ ✷ ✷

I was sipping on my second cup of tea, staring through the cafeteria window at the smoking Tavurvur volcano at the mouth of the Rabaul Harbor, when the seaman marched into the room and informed me that Fujiyama was on the phone.

I hurried off with the aide and was soon in his office speaking with Fujiyama.

"What are you doing on Rabaul?" he asked.

I told him the abbreviated version of the Coral Sea battles, the carrier sinking, and my subsequent rescue from being adrift at sea.

"You're lucky to be alive!"

"I would like to tell you the entire story in person. Very exciting."

"I'd like to hear it, but we're in the middle of a campaign. I don't know if you are aware of the battle we're in here at Guadalcanal."

"I've heard. That's all they talked about at the hospital," I replied. "How goes the effort?"

Fujiyama's mood soured. "The American Marines are putting up stiff resistance since they landed. They've captured the airfield we were building, and we have, so far, been unable to dislodge them." He sighed. "Though we own the night, the Americans are able to bomb our forces and stop our advances on the airfield."

Then he brightened. "The good news is that we have almost eliminated their carrier presence. We sunk the *Hornet* and badly damaged the *Enterprise*. But still, their airfields launch planes at our troops every day."

"The *Hornet*," I mused. "Payback for the Doolittle attack." I thought a moment. "I'll see if can get my editor to let me stay here and report."

"Hai. Do that. That way we could spend some time together and talk." His voice lowered. "Unfortunately, I have bad news. Connor is missing."

139

"What? How?" I barely managed to choke out those two simple words.

"On our way back from the Kobe hospital visiting my wife, the train was hit by an earthquake. Somehow Connor slipped over the embankment and into a raging creek." His voice turned even more solemn. "We've never found him and fear he's dead."

"I'm so sorry," was all I could say. I was saddened by the loss of Connor and for his family. I could see it had greatly affected Fujiyama. After a moment of silence I said, "I'll contact my editor today. I would like to be here for you."

✶ ✶ ✶

"No. Absolutely not. I want you back here," Sakura growled. "We have enough correspondents in the South Pacific Theater as it is. Something big has come up, and I want you to cover it." He was empathic. "Grab some transportation to Tokyo, and get here as quickly as you can." And with that, he hung up.

Internment

"You're getting pretty good at that," noted Counselor General Nagao Kita as he watched Hiyakawa pass a croquet ball through the last hoop on the green of the foreign nationals' internment resort of Montreat.

"Very similar to gateball," Hiyakawa replied. "Our version of croquet. Played a lot of it when I was at school. It helps to keep my mind off Barbara."

"Then I have good news for you," General Kita said with a smile. "A new legal liaison that worked under the Justice Minister arrived today. In a conversation with him, he said he knew something about your wife."

Hiyakawa's eyes lit up. "Is she safe?"

"You'll have to ask him." He waved his hand for Hiyakawa to follow. "I believe he's having lunch at the main house."

Hiyakawa practically pulled Kita along until they finally reached the main dining hall of the resort. Kita surveyed the tables and then escorted Hiyakawa to a Japanese man in his 30s, seated, eating lunch.

"Excuse us," Kita said and bowed. "I would like to introduce someone to you." The young Japanese man, who had a bushy head of black hair and long slender face, looked up from his plate. "Taisei Inoguchi-san this is Kenta Hiyakawa.

"Hai," Inoguchi smiled. "I am happy to meet you. Come. Sit down. Would you like some tea?"

Both men nodded and Inoguchi poured them each a cup of tea.

Hiyakawa got straight to the point. "I apologize for the directness, but do you know the whereabouts of my wife, Barbara Hiyakawa?"

"Well, I know *of* her." Inoguchi ate the last morsel of a cinnamon bun on his plate before continuing. "You see, I am—was—a special legal liaison here in America for the Japanese-Americans living there. Our country sent me and others to help the Japanese with any legal problems they might have. I worked under the authority of Heisuke Yanagawa, Justice Minister and commander of the Tokyo Metropolitan Police."

"How did you find out about my wife?" Hiyakawa pressed.

"Part of my duties was to be informed of any Americans with relatives living in Japan should any trouble with them arise. If so, I would be given a report." He paused a beat. "More tea? Perhaps one of these sweet buns. They are delicious," the bureaucrat offered.

Hiyakawa shook his head.

Inoguchi shrugged. "Anyway, just before the war started a report came across my desk about your wife. It stated she was arrested for sedition."

"Sedition. That's impossible!" Hiyakawa exclaimed.

"Well, she was, and sent to Sugamo prison. You are aware of that prison, yes?"

Hiyakawa nodded.

"What do you know of her now? Anything at all?"

"No more than I just told you. I'm sorry."

"Domo. Domo arigato," Hiyakawa replied. "I appreciate your information."

Kita placed his hands on the diplomat's shoulder. "At least you know where she is. I'm told they will be repatriating some of us soon. Perhaps you may be one of the lucky ones."

One Last Thing to Do

"They're shipping us out," stated a POW private and prison compatriot of Connor's father.

"What? Where?" Williams asked.

"They're shipping us out of this hell-hole," the private replied, "and putting us to work. According to one of the guards, it's at the Hiroshima docks."

"Those Nip bastards," Williams snarled. "Don't put too much credence in the Geneva Convention."

"We're to report in the courtyard in fifteen minutes. Take nothing, the guards said. Just the clothes on your back."

Williams stared past the private, his mind racing. "I have something to do first," Williams said cryptically. "Go ahead. I'll meet you in the courtyard." Williams made his way back to the cellblock and entered the one occupied by Connor and Barbara, but only Connor was inside.

"Where is she?" he growled. "Where's that Jap loving whore?"

"Go to hell," Connor snapped.

Williams walked up to his son, stared at him for a moment, then slapped him hard across the face. "You shouldn't disrespect your father."

Connor rubbed his check and glared at the man that was his father in name only. "You're no kind of father. No kind of man."

Williams' cheeks turned crimson. He reared back and punched the boy straight in the face, sending Connor tumbling backwards and onto the hard concrete floor.

Williams yanked Connor up by his hair, shook him violently enough to snap the boy's head back and forth. "I asked you a question boy. Where's that Jap-whore?"

"Leave him alone," commanded a female voice from the cell entrance.

Williams released Connor unceremoniously to the floor of the cell and turned to Barbara. "Perhaps you heard. I'm being shipped out."

"That's good news," Barbara said. "We won't have to look at your ugly pathetic face anymore."

Williams rushed at Barbara, grabbed her by the neck and pushed her against the cold cell wall. With his other hand, he reached down and ripped her sack dress off in one violent motion.

Williams leered at her nearly naked body, as she stood only in panties and bra. "You'll do just fine. I like skinny women."

"Good for you," Barbara whispered before bringing her knee up and crushing Williams' groin.

Williams collapsed on one knee, moaning in pain, when Connor rushed over and gave him a swift kick to the face. Williams toppled over on his back, grabbing his groin and chin at the same time.

"Run, Barbara," Connor cried. "Get a soldier!"

As Barbara turned to leave, Williams reached up and grabbed her by the leg. She fell face-first onto a bunk, and Williams was on top of her in a flash. Spittle flew from his lips as he ripped off her panties.

Williams unbuckled his pants when he heard something move behind him. He turned just in time to see Connor rushing at him with a wooden chair held over his head. With the instincts of a swift cat, he swung off of his prey and kicked Connor in the stomach.

Connor collapsed to the floor, the chair crashing to the concrete, and gasped for air. He watched as his father picked up the very same chair and brought it down on the crown of his skull.

Connor was out cold.

The interruption dismissed, Williams returned to his amusement.

He flipped Barbara over so that she faced him and beat her mercilessly, punching her again and again in the head until she lost consciousness.

When all resistance ceased, he removed the last shreds of her panties. He stood there a moment, lewdly staring at his prey then unzipped his pants and forcefully mounted her.

Shanghai

I arrived in Tokyo on a cold, grey December day. Though the air temperature wasn't unusually chilly, it was for me. I still had not adjusted to Japanese winter climate after spending a few months in the tropics.

Upon arrival at the Tokyo International Airport, I went directly to my newspaper and found my editor perched as usual behind his desk, wearing his ever-present scowl. "Took you long enough," Sakura snipped.

"After twelve hours and switching planes three times, I'm lucky to be back this soon," I countered.

He waved away the excuse. "We're on a deadline, so don't get comfortable. You leave now." He reached down to his desk drawer. "Here's your military transport voucher to Shanghai."

"Shanghai?!" I gasped. "What's there that's so damn important?"

"You remember those eight Doolittle flyers they captured in China? They've been tried and sentenced under the Enemy Airmen's Act. I want you to get the story for us. The *real* story." He rustled through a stack of random papers, then finally handed me one of his informative dossiers. "Hello and goodbye. Get to it."

Shanghai was an international city with many Europeans living and working there. Brits, Russians, and Dutch to name a few, including many Jews fleeing persecution from Nazi Germany. In

146

addition to the Europeans, there were many Americans residing there as well.

Shanghai had the honor of joining the Japanese Empire right after Pearl Harbor. Shanghai, which literally means the *City on the Sea*, perches on the Yangzi River delta at the point where China's main waterway completes its journey to the Pacific.

I read through Sakura's dossier while on my flight to Shanghai, and as usual, it was pretty thorough. It described the Enemy Airmen's Act in great detail with its articles and sections stipulating that any Allied airmen participating in bombing raids against Japan, or any Japanese-held territory, would be treated as *violators of the law of war* and subjected to trial and punishment if captured by Japanese forces.

Military punishment would either be the death penalty, life imprisonment, or a term of imprisonment for no less than ten years. I wondered what sentence the U.S. Airmen would draw, but deep in my heart, I knew the true answer to that question.

Retributions must be paid.

However, I was not going into the situation blind. Attached to the report was the name of a contact, an American reporter by the name of John Powell. Sakura said they knew each other and to use Powell's name, as the reporter had first-hand knowledge of what was really happening in Shanghai.

Little did I know how *first-hand* it truly was.

I landed at Shanghai's Lunghwa Airport and sought transportation. It was obvious as soon as I arrived that Shanghai was a city under occupation. Japanese soldiers were in the streets making their presence known, and a palpable air of fear permeated the city.

Sakura said I might find John Powell at the ex-pat club called the Shanghai Club, a stately multi-story building noted for its reputed *longest bar in the world*.

I managed to flag down one of the few cabs that were running and made it to The Bund as the club was called. It was a British Club, but all nationalities were welcomed.

As I entered the building, I was impressed with the touted size and length of the ornately carved wooden bar. I couldn't think of any other bar that could compete with it.

"May I help you?" rasped a crackly voice in a British accent. The voice was attached to a tall scarecrow of a man who quickly approached me. The scarecrow wasn't just underweight—his suit hung on him like from a clothesline.

"Yes. I'm looking for an American reporter. John Powell?" Looking very Japanese, I knew he would be suspicious of anything I said.

"Why do you want him? Are you with the police?" he inquired.

"No. No," I stammered. "I'm a reporter for a Tokyo newspaper doing a story on the U.S. Airmen."

He eyed me for a moment, scrutinizing everything about me. "Wait here," he finally instructed.

At that moment, I realized the chatter in the bar ceased and all eyes were turned on me. I felt very uncomfortable even though this was a Japanese occupied city under Japanese rule, and I was pretty sure no harm would come to me. Still, I wondered if I'd have any success with Powell.

The chatter slowly returned, but many of the eyes were still on me, curious to see why I was in their bar. Much to my relief, a middle-aged, bespectacled man with thinning hair approached. He looked haggard, and something about his thin and drawn face looked tortured.

He walked straight up to me and got right to the point. "I'm Powell. You're looking for me?"

"Hai." I corrected myself. "I mean, yes. My editor, Tomoko Sakura, said I should speak with you."

Powell's demeanor softened, and most of his defiance dropped away. "Ah. Tomoko. Is he still chewing on that stupid cigar?"

I nodded. "Always." I cleared my throat and returned Powell's straightforward manner. "I'm here to report on the sentencing of the American fliers. I would like your help, if you're able to provide it."

Powell took a moment or two deciding on a course of action, then pointed to a table in the corner. "Let's sit down and have a drink."

After reaching our seats, I got right to the point. "I need background on the occupation first."

"I could assume what happened here—what *is* happening here—is not reported well in the Japanese press," he said, using chosen words.

"The persecution of the Chinese," I interjected. "I saw what the Japanese did in Singapore."

"This is worse. And I'm not bigoted against the Chinese. I came here to live and run a newspaper called the *China Weekly Review*. But the Japanese here are far harsher on nationals. British, Americans and Dutch. We slowly lost our privileges and had to wear letters—B, A, or N—when walking in public places. Our villas were turned into brothels and gambling houses. Many of us are being interned in concentration camps."

He raised his hand to the bartender. "Tea? Or something stronger?"

"Tea is fine," I replied.

"Two teas," Powell shouted, then turned his attention back to me. "It was bad enough with the Japanese Army, but in November of this year, it got even worse, which I never thought possible." Powell's eyebrows knitted, and I could see the hate in his eyes. "The Kempeitai came to Shanghai."

The tea arrived, and Powell poured a cup for both of us.

"Roundups began almost immediately. The Kempeitai launched early morning raids, arresting hundreds of Britons, Americans, Dutch, and some other foreign nationals." He scoffed at the thought. "They were labeled *Prominent Citizens* and hauled off to Haiphong Road Camp, a hellhole of a place, run by the Imperial Japanese Army."

He was quiet for a moment as I sat there, sipping on my tea, waiting for him to continue. Finally, he sighed. "From their record of cruelty in China and Singapore, we knew we were going to suffer indescribable ill-treatment, which we did indeed." He pointed out the window to the east. "Many of us were taken to Bridge House, a large apartment complex just across Garden Bridge. It became the main interrogation and torture center for the Kempeitai."

He stared into his tea, and his voice quivered when he spoke again. "The Kempeitai arrested many foreign journalists, businessmen, and police officers. Some were held for months. Beaten, whipped, given the water torture, electrocuted, and starved. It was brutal."

I noticed his hands grip his tea tighter. "The outspoken British editor of *Oriental Affairs*, my good friend, who had attacked the Japanese for their earlier outrages in China, almost died at the hands of the Kempeitai. Sir Frederick Maze, former inspector-general of Chinese Customs, was tortured for weeks before finally being released without a charge. Anyone even remotely suspected of being anti-Japanese was arrested and tortured. The fear of a knock on the door in the middle of the night was literal."

"And you?" I hesitated. "Were you arrested?"

His resulting laughter was mixed with disdain. "My newspaper was deemed treasonous. So the Kempeitai arrested me and beat me mercilessly." He rolled up the sleeves of his jacket and the trousers of his pants, revealing hideous scars on his legs and arms. "These are nothing compared to my back and private areas."

I had nothing to say. What could I say?

"Anyway, you wanted background. I gave it to you," he grunted.

I finally found my voice. "What about the airmen? Will they get the death penalty?"

Powell reached into his worn jacket and pulled out a slip of paper. "This was given to me by an associate of mine. I can't say whom—for his sake. These are the names of all eight of the Americans who were sentenced to death."

He handed me the ragged document. "But for some odd reason known only to the Japanese, only three are to be executed. Two pilots and a gunner. They are accused of strafing and bombing civilian buildings and a grammar school."

"When is their execution?"

He almost laughed. "You're just in time. This evening. If you want to report on it, go to the City Police Headquarters were they're being held. I assume they will be shot before the day is done."

Tried and Sentenced

W hen I arrived at Police Headquarters, the waiting area was packed with news reporters. This was big news in Japan, and it was going to be well covered.

The cadre of reporters had been waiting for several hours. I stood next to an elderly Japanese man with a neatly trimmed goatee and asked, "Did they set a time for the execution?"

"Hai," he replied. "In one hour. We will be—"

A stout Japanese sergeant interrupted our conversation. "I am Sergeant Shotaro in charge of the execution. Trucks are out front. They will take all news personnel to the cemetery. Please board immediately."

"Cemetery?" I said.

"Hai," the goateed man responded. "An old Chinese cemetery outside of town."

As we headed out of the city, and the day turned to dusk, a strange reddish glow appeared on the horizon as if the lifeblood of the day was passing before us.

We rolled up to the burial ground dotted with small shrines. I had not been to a Chinese cemetery and was surprised to see these strange little sanctuaries. But they were not your ordinary burial plots.

Each family that could afford the expense had a complete shrine for their loved ones. Most were equipped with a small kitchen and bathroom for occasions when the family came to visit. Some contained oil paintings of the departed while others had tiny patios with flowers. There were a series of streets throughout the cemetery, and the entire area looked like a neighborhood for the dead.

We exited the trucks, and Sergeant Shotaro guided us through the cemetery to an area in the back near some rough terrain. A handful of mangy dogs were scavenging in front of us, but were chased off by our guide.

I noticed a line of several Japanese infantry standing erect with rifles at their side. Moments later, we heard a rustling of feet, and three malnourished Americans appeared before us.

They looked dour, yet stoic. If they felt fear, their demeanor did not reveal it. In fact, they seemed resigned to their fate. In some respects, as a Japanese-American, I felt some pride in the way these Americans nobly faced their own deaths.

The three Americans were hustled over in front of the line of armed soldiers, and towards three wooden crosses erected in the ground. Each of the condemned was placed in front of one of the crosses, forced to their knees, and tied to the cross. Finally, black sacks were placed over their heads.

A few of the infantrymen fidgeted with the stock of their rifles, impatiently waiting for what had become a ritual for them. When the condemned were in position, and without time to collect my thoughts, I heard Sergeant Shotaro bark out an order. "Ready."

The soldiers briskly brought the stocks of their rifles to their shoulders.

"Aim."

The crowd of spectators and my fellow journalists turned deathly silent.

"*Fire!*"

A volley of bullets cut into the bound bodies of the American prisoners, and in a matter of seconds, the bloody corpses slumped over, deprived of life.

"That is all. Follow me back to the trucks," Sergeant Shotaro stated as if this horrendous act meant nothing.

I hesitated for a moment to glimpse the three bodies being untied and flung onto a make-shift cart like sacks of waste. I harbored an inner-thought that I dared not share with anyone.

I hope the Japanese officers who illegally sentenced these Americans to death will be found guilty of war crimes some day.

I'm Sorry My Friend

Yoshi, suffering from malnutrition and exhaustion, as were the remainder of his company, looked at a torn calendar page he found in his box of meager personal belongings. It would make a good patch for the sole of his rotting boot that had become decimated by jungle rot and insects.

He glanced at the slip of paper before inserting it into his boot. The date was December 1942, and he realized he had been on Guadalcanal for months that felt more like years. Terrible years he wanted to forget.

Private Tanaka, a young member of his platoon, looked upon the carcass of a dog they had killed on the beach. As they had no other food options, the platoon intended to dine on the meat. Maggots had already ravaged the flesh. It didn't matter to Yoshi. He was suffering from a bout of dysentery, and meat would only make it worse. No cooking fires were permitted so all meals were to be uncooked and cold.

Tanaka shredded the meat of the dog with a blunt knife without speaking a word to Yoshi. His sullen eyes were like that of the other troops—full of resignation; of lost hope.

The soldiers had taken to referring to Guadalcanal as *Starvation Island*, a pun derived from the first phoneme in the Japanese name for the island. But the pun had lost its humor as hunger, jungle fever, and malaria afflicted each and every soldier.

The only relief from all this suffering came in the form of sake.

The troops drank the ample supply of the rice liquor that flowed, and along with the intoxication, the conversation flowed as well. One soldier, who had a bizarre sense of humor, crawled over a small group of his drunken comrades, dropped his pants, and pointed to his bare ass. "If I die," he joked, "go ahead and eat this part."

Yoshi, along with the other soldiers, laughed at the man's public display. But the moment of levity was short-lived for Yoshi. "The Army doctors will not even send us to the rear, no matter how sick we are."

Tanaka agreed. "I fear we're left to die from exhaustion and malnutrition, rather than from bullets."

Yoshi looked around the remaining men of his company who downed glass after glass of sake. "I've heard we are planning a final push on the American airfield, but how do they expect us to fight with drunk soldiers?"

Tanaka nodded his head. "Another Banzai. That's why the sake."

"Hai," Yoshi replied. "I think you're right." He had heard of such things. Drunken or drugged soldiers running blindly into enemy fire screaming "Banzai" at the top of their lungs.

Yoshi and Tanaka helped themselves to more sake when Gima, a university student turned soldier, dropped beside them and mused. "You know how a lion kills, Yoshi?"

"What? A lion?"

"Hai." Gima sucked down his remaining cup of sake. "When a lion charges, it roars and attempts to use its bulk as a battering ram in order to send its prey reeling."

"And that's your explanation of a Banzai charge?"

Gima nodded. "A lion devours nothing it has not first charged."

The brief conversation and respite from reality came to a grinding halt when Sergeant Gunso barked. "Everyone. Move out!"

"This is it," Gima said in resignation as he fell in with Yoshi and the remainder of the Company. "For honor and glory."

Yoshi and his company took up their positions on the edge of a bamboo forest and awaited the coming of night because U.S. Marines had dug in on the other side of the thick sprawl of foliage.

The air stood quiet and still, almost peaceful, as Yoshi watched the sun, now a dark red disk against a dusk sky, set behind the mountains miles away. It reminded him of the flag of his nation. Was it possible that his country, too, was about to set?

Sergeant Gunso walked amongst his troops, speaking quietly but sternly. "Off your asses! Let's move! Pass it on down the line."

The unit slowly stood up and walked carefully over the rocky ground with fingers pressed to their triggers. As they crossed a small patch of open field lit only by the moonlight, a cry of, "Banzai," came out of the darkness, followed by the calls of, "Marine you die," and, "Blood for the Emperor." The company, now joined by the remnants of their battalion, started to rush blindly across the field.

Suddenly a starburst shell exploded high above them. Then another and another, illuminating the entire night landscape. The whole unit ran screaming and yelling, "Banzai," in the hopes of inciting fear in the enemy.

The starburst shells overhead were replaced by a hail of projectiles plowing into their ranks, raking the front columns of the attack with machine gun fire, cutting bloody swaths into their lines.

Yoshi's head snapped to his left then to his right, and he saw the horror of his fellow troops being shredded by small, razor-sharp missiles fired from the tree line in front of them at point-blank range. But despite the carnage around him, Yoshi kept running forward, firing bursts from his rifle and racing past fallen comrades. The chatter of machine guns, the screams of the mortally wounded, and the concussion of mortar shells filled the air.

Added to this melee of death, came a barrage of artillery fire that dropped round after round of shrapnel and phosphorous shells on an already decimated attacking infantry. The sounds of anguish filled the night as the shrapnel cut into their ranks and phosphorous landed on exposed skin, searing the hot chemical into their flesh.

Groups of men crumbled under the barrage of artillery fire around him, but Yoshi managed to make it to the tree line of palms. He crouched down for cover and heard someone moan just in front of him.

He spotted Gima twisting on the ground next to a shell hole. As he stumbled to assist his comrade, Yoshi stopped short in revulsion. The lower half of his friend's body, his legs and feet, had been blown off.

As Yoshi stood there speechless, Gima moaned desperately. "Kill me. Please kill me, Yoshi."

Yoshi knew there was no saving his friend, but his thoughts were conflicted over the grim request. He steeled himself and spoke softly, "Gomen'nasai. I'm sorry, my friend." And he discharged his rifle.

He had little time to mourn when a shell burst above him, shattering the top of a palm tree. First, he felt staggering pain shoot along his thigh. Then he looked up to see a mass of palm fronds and chunks of wood fall upon him, burying him with debris.

An inky pool of darkness crept in from the edges of his vision as Yoshi slipped into unconsciousness.

Lost Cause

It was the end of December when Fujiyama marched down the tubular concrete re-enforced tunnel that led to Yamamoto's underground bunker at Rabaul for the daily conference. The bunker was part of an elaborate system of tunnels and caverns dug into the hillside to protect against air attacks. The cool damp air of the tunnel was a welcome respite from the stifling heat outside.

Fujiyama sensed that this was to be a decisive conference. The news from Guadalcanal was bad—all bad. The soldiers on the island had failed to pry the U.S. Marines from Henderson Field where the constant air attacks prevented the Japanese Navy from properly re-supplying the Army on the island. The Army had lost two-thirds of the soldiers committed in the battle—over 35,000 men.

The naval reversals were even worse. The sea battles of mid-November had cost the Japanese countless ships and planes without achieving any of their objectives. But by far, the most significant loss was the decimation of the elite group of naval aviators.

And there was a more personal note.

Fujiyama knew Yoshi served on Guadalcanal, and as conditions there worsened, he had become increasingly more concerned with his son's safety on the island. Yoshi's letters home indicated a growing sense of doom that was reflected by the events on the island. As far as his eldest son was concerned, Fujiyama's inquiries indicated he had survived the battle of Midway, and as with other

Midway pilots, was being held incognito to prevent the public from knowing the extent of the military disaster.

With the thoughts of his sons racing through his mind, Fujiyama entered the concrete bunker to see Ugaki and Yamamoto staring at a map that plotted worldwide domination.

He seated himself next to Ugaki, and both officers waited for their Admiral to speak. They could see he was clearly despondent in the way he held himself—the very expression of defeat etched upon his face. They had failed to dislodge the Americans from Guadalcanal, and Yamamoto had a critical decision to make. He had to rethink his strategy of forming a larger south Pacific ring that protected the Empire. He also knew the chances now of capturing the Solomon Islands, advancing on Fuji, Samoa, New Caledonia, and even Australia, were close to nil.

The silence in the bunker hung thick like the toxic air as minutes clicked by.

Yamamoto finally spoke.

"I'm going to Tokyo very soon. I have petitioned Prime Minister Tojo to withdraw from Guadalcanal and to evacuate the Army. I will speak with the Emperor for his permission, of course."

Ugaki and Fujiyama were not surprised at Yamamoto's announcement. Guadalcanal *was* a lost cause—lost through logistics alone. The Japanese were never able to replace their losses as well as the Americans.

"Draw up plans for the withdrawal," he said with finality and curtly dismissed the two officers.

Withdrawal

"Y**ou're** leaving," Sergeant Gunso informed Yoshi. "You have a concussion, but it's the bullet that shattered your thigh bone that's your one-way ticket out of here."

Yoshi was lying atop a stretcher on the beach, and although he had been in and out of consciousness, he was slowly regaining his wits.

"I'm being evacuated?"

"Hai. And rumor has it everyone is as well."

"Everyone?" Yoshi choked out. "We lost the island?"

"I don't control strategy, Corporal," Gunso snapped. "But anyone with a pair of eyes can see the Americans still control the island." He stared towards the jungle. "I believe we're through, and I think the Generals and Admirals see that, too."

He looked down at Yoshi's leg held in a splint. "Anyway, it's a sure thing for you. The barges are coming now to pick up the wounded." He pointed to bloated, black corpses scattered here and there, stacked atop bonfires like firewood. "And the ashes of our dead."

Yoshi gagged against the sickening stench. Burning muscle tissue gave off an aroma similar to beef in a frying pan, and charred body fat smelled like a side of fatty pork on the grill.

Gunso pointed out toward the sea. "The barges may attract U.S. planes. We need to get you loaded on as quickly as possible."

Several minutes later, a handful of barges hit the beach with blunt impact and dropped their front doors sending foam and sea water spiraling into the air.

The crew of the barges disembarked like swarms of flies, hurried forward and picked up the wounded one group at a time, always with an eye to the skies.

Two soldiers assisted Yoshi to his feet and moved toward one of the barges when the familiar sound of airplane engines crackled through the air. After months on the island, Yoshi knew that sound well.

Fighter planes.

Yoshi was essentially tossed aboard the barge and seated on the cold metal floor when overhead, he could hear the sound of planes quickly losing altitude. He struggled to his feet, looked up at the sky, and then to the beach.

Three U.S. Marine F4F fighters swooped down and strafed the shoreline, sending clouds of white sand spouting like small eruptions into air. The lines of machine gun bullets went right through the men on the beach, many of which were wounded and unable to find cover.

Yoshi watched as Sergeant Gunso pulled a wounded man toward the tree line, only to be cut down by tracer bullets.

The F4Fs now turned their attention to the barges that had set out to sea, but this was to be no strafing run.

Gunners on the barges fired at the approaching planes, trying their best to hit their targets, but to no avail. The fighters flew in formation and once they were over the near-helpless barges, bombs dropped one-by-one.

The barge directly in front of Yoshi's received a direct hit. Flames, twisted metal and bodies flew like confetti. The young machine gunner on Yoshi's barrage fired frantically at the attacking fighter and finally managed a hit. Smoke trailed from the underbelly of the F4F, but the plane kept its course, and released a bomb directly over its target.

Yoshi looked up as the dark object dropped closer and closer and directly toward his barge.

An earsplitting explosion erupted just behind the barge, and Yoshi felt his body blown into the deep waters. He floated amongst the undulating waves, surrounded by the smell of burning fuel and men screaming in pain. He tried desperately to tread water, but his splint prevented him for staying afloat.

His head sank below the surface as his weight dragged him deeper into the ocean's depths.

Unable to break the surface, he gasped his last breath, and his lungs filled with water instead as he was consumed by a watery grave.

Hatching A Plot

On a cold, blustery day in February of 1943, Yamamoto rode the short distance from Naval Headquarters to the Emperor's Palace for a meeting of the Imperial Council. The Council only met in rare moments of special importance when major decisions were to be made—like the invasion of China, and now, the Greater East Asia War.

Yamamoto expected the mood of the Council to be as cold as the weather, and he was not disappointed.

"Your aggressive tactics on fighting the war has failed," Prince Chichibu bluntly stated as soon as the other Council members were seated. Sitting on both sides of the Prince were Emperor Hirohito, Prime Minister Tojo, and other high ranking members of the Naval General Staff.

"First Midway; now Guadalcanal," Chichibu continued with an accusatory finger. "With the luxury of hindsight, you can now see the wisdom of the defensive posture of the Naval General Staff." He looked at the Emperor then back to Yamamoto. "So, tell us. What are your plans now?"

Yamamoto glanced at Hirohito, avoiding the Prince altogether.

"As with the disaster at Midway, I apologize again, Your Majesty, for my failure at Guadalcanal. It has turned into a battle of attrition. A battle my command could not sustain with such great losses of men, aircraft, and ships. But we *did* achieve an extremely important tactical victory. Soon after Prime Minister

Tojo gave me permission, we successfully evacuated 13,000 of our troops."

The Emperor did not speak, as was the norm at the Council meetings, leaving it up to the other members to comment on.

Chichibu ignored this information and pressed Yamamoto further. "So. Now you will have to rethink your strategy of forming a larger South Pacific ring protecting the Empire. Correct?"

Yamamoto ignored Chichibu and once again focused his attention upon the Emperor. "Though we've lost Guadalcanal, we must keep the Solomon Islands. I have my staff working on plans to do just that. Meanwhile, I will personally conduct an inspection tour to boost moral of the troops there."

"*That* is your plan?" Chichibu snipped. "A goodwill tour of the South Pacific?"

Yamamoto finally had enough of the Prince's condescension. "I informed this very Council that if war came with America, the way to keep her at bay, was to demoralize her and establish an aggressive posture," he scolded. "Time and again, we've underestimated the ability of the Americans to bounce back and retaliate. We wrongly assumed that America would continue to be weak, that they would fold, and as a result, we had few plans to meet possible American counterstrikes." He leveled a look directly at Chichibu. "I warned of this at the start."

Tojo pounded his fist to the table. "Enough!" He directly addressed the Prince. "We agree, as does Admiral Yamamoto, that we will strengthen our defensive ring and defend against the Americans and their allies until factors more in our favor present themselves."

With that, the Emperor stood, and the meeting was disbanded.

Outside, on the street facing the Palace, Chichibu discretely met with Sato. Both men had their collars up, not only to protect themselves from the cold wind, but also their words from prying ears

"The war is going badly for the Axis," said Sato. "The Germans were stopped at Leningrad. Both they and the Italians are being pushed out of North Africa as we speak. And now Yamamoto has gone from disagreement with the war to defeatist."

"His counsel is too close to His Majesty," the Prince added. "Something must be done."

"Perhaps Yamamoto has handed us an opportunity," Sato said slyly.

The Prince nodded, then smiled. "Perhaps. Perhaps he has."

Reunion

Hiyakawa arrived at the Tokyo airport on a cold March day in 1943. Being newly repatriated, his duty demanded that he report to his office. But he had other plans. He broke away from the crowd of other repatriated passengers and wasted no time in calling a cab to head directly to the prison where Barbara was being held.

After a short trip from the airport that felt like an eternity, he rolled up in front of Sugamo prison. He quickly paid the cab driver and raced towards the guard office.

The prison's walls loomed above him and cast a depressing mood over Hiyakawa. It turned his stomach to think his lovely, cultured wife had to endure such a vile place.

He was determined, though. Determined to have Barbara released no matter what and no matter how. He would use every bit of influence he had in order to gain her freedom and be reunited with his loving partner.

"My name is Kenta Hiyakawa. Assistant to the Lord Keeper of the Privy Seal," he declared to the civilian guard behind a small, wooden desk.

The guard scratched his goatee and gave Hiyakawa a confused look. Hiyakawa's position meant nothing to him.

"Do you know who I am? I represent the Emperor," the diplomat boomed in his most authoritative voice. "I'm here for my wife. I want to see her immediately. Here are my credentials," Hiyakawa barked, thrusting his wallet in the guard's face.

But before the guard could reply, a Japanese infantry officer, a young captain, stepped into the office. "What's going on here? What's the trouble?"

Hiyakawa showed his credentials once again to the young captain. "I want to see my wife, Barbara Hiyakawa."

The captain looked over Hiyakawa's I.D., then simply handed it back to him and stated with no empathy at all. "She's dead."

Hiyakawa's legs felt as if they buckled from under him. "Dead... when...how?"

"She died several weeks ago. Cracked her skull against the floor of her cell. Her body was claimed by her family or friends, I don't know whom."

Despair mixed with misery flooded over Hiyakawa while the officer impatiently waited, emotionless, for his next question.

But Hiyakawa just stood there devastated. Overwhelmed with grief. "Hurt her head? That's all you know?"

The officer sighed, impatient and inconvenienced. "There was a young boy in her cell with her at the time. He might know more. Would you like to see him?"

Hiyakawa couldn't form words, so he simply nodded instead.

The grieving husband followed the officer down the grimy halls of a nearby cellblock that only made Hiyakawa feel even more sickened. For his lovely wife to die in such filthy and wretched surroundings was almost too much for him to bear.

The officer stopped in front of a cell that looked like all the others. "This was her cell."

Hiyakawa looked past the officer and into the small space. It smelled of mold and rot, and sitting upon one of the bunks was Connor. "Connor-san! What are *you* doing here?"

Hiyakawa stepped into the cell and sat next to the American boy. "Do you remember me?"

Connor stared at the diplomat for a few seconds then nodded his head. "Yes. I remember. I met you in our home in the U.S." He licked at dry lips before continuing. "You're Barbara's husband?"

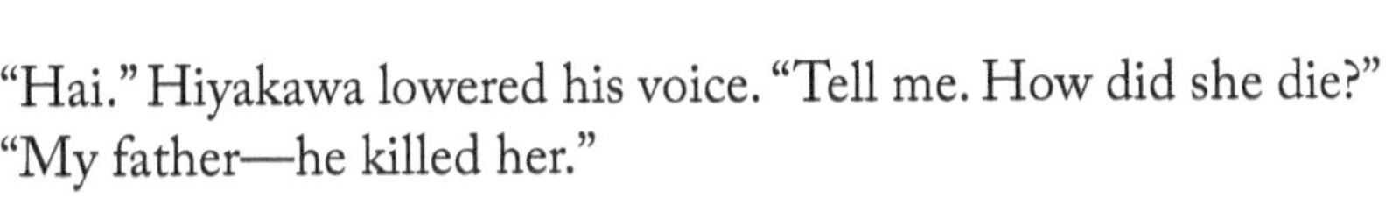

"Hai." Hiyakawa lowered his voice. "Tell me. How did she die?"

"My father—he killed her."

"*Fujiyama??*"

"No. My *real* father. My American father. He came here as a POW." Tears streaked down Connor's filthy face. "My father—he's evil. He tormented us both. But your wife, Barbara, always tried to protect me. No matter what the cost. Then, one night, he came into our cell...and he-he raped her. Then he murdered her."

Hiyakawa's head was spinning. This was too much information for him to absorb in such a short time, but somehow he managed to find the words to speak to Connor. "Where is your father now?"

"I don't know."

Hiyakawa was quiet for a few minutes then said, "I've got to get you home once they know who you are."

"Your wife tried, but they wouldn't listen to her."

The little diplomat stood erect and stated with a resolute voice, "They *will* listen to me."

A Sad Homecoming

Hong Kong, Manila, Singapore, New Guinea, and the Solomon Islands once sparkled as signposts on the perimeter of the Great East Asia Co-Prosperity Sphere, but were now only sad markers to Japanese survivors that returned to their homeland.

Trains that once carried confident, joyous soldiers to the front, now carried the ashes of the dead that lost their lives defending foreign lands they believed was theirs to keep.

As the trains journeyed through the many prefectures, the ritual of sending off troops was reversed.

Fujiyama, notified of his son's death, was permitted to accompany his son's ashes back home to Hiroshima. There, family members, local officials, reservists, and representatives of the same patriotic organizations that sent the young men off to war with rousing orations, met the remains at train stations and marched with them solemnly back to the neighborhoods.

As difficult as it was, Hiryo could not attend the funeral of his own brother. Fujiyama explained to Miyoko that Hiryo was not permitted to leave the Imperial Navy logistical base that served as the operating home base for the Imperial Japanese Navy's Combined Fleet. Fujiyama was forced to lie to his wife, telling her that Hiryo was training pilots, not because he and other survivors of the disaster at Midway were being sequestered from the Japanese public.

As Kenji waited for his father to disembark the train with Yoshi's ashes, he turned to his mother with a perplexed expression. "Mama-san, how many more spirits will we be welcoming home?"

Miyoko knew what he meant and was struck with the thought—*Will I be standing here some day awaiting Hiryo's ashes?*

When the train pulled into the station, the families of the war dead rushed toward the cars, somberly waiting to receive boxes containing all that remained of their loved ones. Shortly, a soldier wearing white gloves and a mask covering his mouth, passed a *shiraki no hako*—a white cotton cloth covered box—through the train window. Other soldiers began this process as well, passing box after box to family members who rushed to retrieve them.

Most clung to the wooden boxes and openly wept.

Several minutes later, Miyoko saw her husband step off the train carrying his own *shiraki no hako*. Fujiyama was dressed in the full regalia of the Japanese Naval Staff Office. Miyoko had seen this uniform many times before, but now it had one change. A third gold stripe had been added to his shoulder boards.

Fujiyama approached Kenji, Suki, and his wife, clutching the small box in front of him that contained his son and their brother. He remained stoic, as did his family, at least until the burial was complete, and they were in the privacy of their own home.

The procession of the dead to the city's cemetery lasted a few hours, and Yoshi's ashes were interned in the family plot. Not a single word was exchanged throughout the somber journey and memorial.

As they returned home, Kenji saw an addition to the Japanese Naval Flag that waved over their house. A black streamer had been added to indicate that a man had been called to colors. On a small table by the front door, a *Gunbjin Izoku Kisho*—the Soldier's Bereaved Family Medal—a small silver medallion bearing the Imperial Chrysanthemum suspended from a looped, cross-shaped, dark purple tassel.

Miyoko scowled at the medal.

Next to it was the official monetary compensation issued to

families of the dead. "Thirty yen. Thirty yen for the life of my son to the Emperor." She ripped the envelope in half. "Thirty yen for my baby."

Fujiyama placed his arm around his grieving wife but said nothing.

As Miyoko rested her head on his chest, she touched his shoulder board," You have your third gold stripe. You've been promoted."

"Hai. To Captain." But there was no pride or sense of accomplishment in his voice.

After eating a light supper of food and drink prepared by the women of the neighborhood, Fujiyama stood from the table and addressed his family. "Tomorrow your mother and I go to Tokyo to enshrine Yoshi in the Yasukuni Shrine that honor the war dead." He paused a moment and spoke directly to Kenji and Suki. "After that, I will not be coming home. I leave Tokyo with Admiral Yamamoto soon after the ceremony."

His children didn't ask any questions or protest against his duties. They merely stood and walked to their rooms without speaking.

Easing the Pain

"*Connor is alive?!*" Suki's excited voice shouted over the phone.

"Hai. I have him here with me in Tokyo," Hiyakawa said. "May I speak to Fujiyama?"

"He and my mother are not here. They are in Tokyo as well. They left this morning." She went on to tell of the tragic news of Yoshi's death and the processional.

Hiyakawa had no words of comfort for Suki, except to say that he was sorry for the tragic loss.

"Tell me the good news," she said softly. "Tell me of Connor."

"He's here with me in my office. I'll let you speak to him." He handed the phone to Connor who after a brief, tearful greeting, told the astonished girl everything he had conveyed to Hiyakawa.

"Your own father?" Suki replied in shock. "He killed Hiyakawa's wife!?"

Connor went on to tell Suki all the ugly details. All, that is, except for Connor's newly discovered ancestry. Connor was determined to reserve that bit of news for a personal conversation with Fujiyama.

"Suki," Hiyakawa said after retrieving the phone from Connor. "We'll look for your parents at the shrine today. I trust that Connor's return will ease some of their pain."

Yasukuni Jinja

"**R**epatriated?" I said as I sat in front of my editor's desk.

"Hai," Sakura mumbled over his cigar. "Came in with a group of repatriates yesterday. All top administrators and such."

"Well, that's good news. Very good news."

"And thus your next assignment. You're in good with Hiyakawa, and I wish you to get a first-person interview with him. It will make for good copy."

"But I just flew in from Shanghai. I need some rest."

"Rest later. You did a good story on those American flyers, but I need you to get on this before any of the other papers get the story. The public would love to know what it felt like to be in the clutches of our notorious enemy."

I was tired and desperately needed a bath, but I resigned myself to Sakura's wishes. "Hai. I'll call his office and ask for the interview."

I had one visit to do first. I left quickly for the Yasukuni Shrine.

✳ ✳ ✳

"There it is," noted Fujiyama to Miyoko. He pointed to the top of a hill near the Imperial Palace. "Yoshi's spirit will reside in the Yasukuni Jinja. The national memorial to the war dead." He tried his best to put on a brave front and sooth the pain of his distressed wife. "His spirit will rest with the spirits of 2.5 million war dead dating back to the mid-1800s. He will become a national deity. A *kami*."

But Miyoko remained silent. She had lost her precious baby, and in her mind, being a deity was small compensation for the sacrifice of her precious son.

Betrayal

After the enshrinement ceremony of Yoshi's spirit, Fujiyama and Miyoko hailed a cab to return to the railway station. As a cab pulled to the curb, and they were about to climb inside, Fujiyama felt a light touch on his shoulder.

"Commander?"

Fujiyama turned to see Hiyakawa standing before him. It took him a moment to process before speaking. "What are you doing here? I thought you were interned in America?"

"I was just repatriated. I arrived yesterday."

Fujiyama heard the utter sadness in Hiyakawa's voice. "That's great news."

Hiyakawa gave him a feeble nod. "I found out where Barbara was. She was arrested by the Kempeitai and sent to Sugamo prison. I went to release her only to find that she was dead. Murdered."

Fujiyama, shocked at what he heard, quickly dismisses the waiting cab and ushered Hiyakawa and Miyoko back to the sidewalk. "Murdered? How?"

Hiyakawa told the grisly story of Barbara's confinement and murder but withheld the information of Connor and his father. "And there's something else." He looked directly at Miyoko. "Something I hope will lift your spirits." He motioned towards the other side of the street, waving to Connor and myself.

As it turned out, I found Connor at the Shrine when I went searching for Hiyakawa.

When Miyoko saw us, her heart soared. "Connor-san!" she cried, running directly into rush hour traffic trying to reach her prodigal son.

Connor easily scooped the small woman in his arms and rescued her from passing cars, and brought her back to the safety of the sidewalk.

"Oh, Connor-san! Connor-san." His adopted mother wept for both her sons, the living and the dead.

I smiled at seeing the bittersweet family reunion. Fujiyama turned to me. "And how is it that you are here?"

"I wanted to ask Hiyakawa for an interview now that he was repatriated, and his office told me he would be here at the shrine."

"And you came to return our son as well," Miyoko said with a tear and a smile. "Domo. Domo arigato."

During all of this, I noticed that Connor appeared somewhat detached and seemed uncomfortable when looking at Fujiyama. Then, when Fujiyama placed his hand on Connor's shoulder, the teen recoiled.

"What's wrong?" Fujiyama asked.

"Did they tell you who killed Hiyakawa's wife?" Conner snapped. "It was *my* father."

Fujiyama stared at Connor slack-faced, unable to find the words to respond.

"It's true, Commander," Hiyakawa said. "Williams is responsible for Barbara's murder."

Connor moved closer to Fujiyama, challenging his Japanese father. "Maybe he's an evil bastard, but at least he told the truth. He admitted killing my mother for being Japanese and..."

Fujiyama stared into Connor's eyes that burned with utter contempt. "Why didn't you tell me that I'm half-Japanese? Why didn't Mieko? Why didn't you tell me the truth of who I am?"

Fujiyama once again tried to reach out and touch his son, but Connor would have no part of it. "You have every right to be angry. But it was Mieko who made me swear on her deathbed not to tell you," Fujiyama replied weakly. "She felt you were already being treated as an outcast, and adding the knowledge that you were Japanese living in a bigoted America would only make your life worse. I didn't want to hurt you."

"But then I came to Japan. Why didn't you tell me then?"

Miyoko interjected softly. "Connor-san. We talked about telling you, but your mother was Ainu. A Japanese ethnic group seen as outcasts. You were already an ijin here, and by the time Fujiyama and I agreed to tell you, the war with America began."

"And if we told you then," Fujiyama said, "You would be seen as not only an ijin, but as a traitor as well, and your life would be in danger."

None of this placated Connor. The pain of his life, the lies he lived both in Japan and America were too great to be comforted by their empty words and intentions.

"You talk of the Samurai code. Samurai loyalty and Samurai honor," Connor raged directly at Fujiyama. "And you have *neither*! You...you..." he suddenly began to gag uncontrollably. He clutched at his stomach, his eyes widening, then collapsed to the sidewalk at his Japanese parents' feet.

An Invitation

"I think we caught it in time," the surgeon informed the Fujiyamas at the Tokyo Isen, one of the oldest medical schools of Japan. The surgeon was an elderly man, wearing wire rim glasses and a white lab coat with a stethoscope peeking from his side pocket.

The Fujiyamas were seated in a waiting area near Connor's room and hung on the doctor's every word. "The boy is very lucky that his appendix didn't burst," the surgeon admitted.

"May we see him now?" asked Fujiyama.

"Hai," the surgeon replied. "But he *must* have peace and quiet. It's imperative that he remains stable."

Miyoko touched Fujiyama's arm. "Perhaps it's best that I see him alone."

Fujiyama didn't argue the point. He just prayed that he could repair his relationship with his son after he healed. "Did you call your sister? Did she agree to take Connor in for a while?"

"Hai. They should be here soon, but I will ask Connor-san if he'd like to stay with them. It's important that he's given the choice." She stood and quietly entered the door to Connor's room.

Connor and Miyoko were speaking together when they heard a gentle knock on at the door. A Japanese woman, a little older than Miyoko, entered the room along with a much younger woman.

"You remember my sister, Mai," Miyoko said.

"Kon'nichiwa, Connor-san," Mai bowed in reply.

But Connor's attention was on the young woman at Mai's side. Her exquisiteness stunned him to silence. He had yet to see such beauty, such loveliness in a woman in all his years living in Japan. Her long, shiny black hair fell upon a short, thin body. Her porcelain skin was impossibly white, unlined, and flawless.

Mai tried to repress a smile from Connor's awe. "This is Aiko. My daughter."

Aiko smiled and bowed her head.

"Miyoko would like you to accept our invitation for you to stay with us in Tokyo while you recover. Aiko and I would be honored if you accepted."

Still staring at Aiko, Connor stammered, his mouth agape. "Umm... Hai. Domo." What else could he say? Just to be in the presence of such beauty was going to be a treat and might even help him temporarily forget the betrayal he felt.

A Gold Lead

"A resort? An actual resort!" I stammered in surprise.

"Hai," Hiyakawa replied. I interviewed him in his office next to the Lord Keeper of the Privy Seal. The peaceful and chaste environment of traditional Japanese décor matched that of the gentleness of the man himself. The walls were painted in neutral colors, and a simple, uncluttered maple desk accentuated the geometric order of Japanese design. Two simple statues perched on pedestals, and large watercolor prints decorated the walls, giving a Zen-like atmosphere to the room.

"Then your stay was peaceful and trouble-free?" I inquired.

"On the whole, yes. The only friction we encountered was between the Japanese themselves."

"In what way?"

"As you well know, Japanese society is very structured with the classes clearly divided. This was not the case at the resort. All mixes of class were thrown together there—diplomats, politicos, businessmen, women and children. The Americans treated all of us as mutually equal."

"Ah. I could see how that would get under the skin of the more *privileged* classes," I chuckled.

Hiyakawa nodded before his civil mood shifted. "I should clarify that, we, as expatriates were treated regally. Not so with the Japanese–Americans."

"We have heard very little news of how they were being treated.

I warned my parents of that when I visited before the war, but they wouldn't believe me. And I feared for them."

"Your fears are well founded," he said solemnly. "In fact, I came upon your family as we passed through California."

"You did?"

"Hai. They appeared in good health and were being sent to an internment camp. I couldn't speak with them long, but they told me to tell you they were well and to send you their love."

My thoughts were my own for a few moments, hoping my parents would make it through this wretched conflict. I had little idea how they were being treated, only hearing the propaganda from our government. I made a promise to myself to return to America once the war ended and rejoin my family.

My reflections were interrupted when Hiyakawa said, "There's one other thing. Something I think you might be interested in."

"Oh? And what's that?"

"I've had infrequent discussions with Fujiyama. On one occasion, he told me of your interest in stolen gold."

"Go on," I said, my ears perking up.

"Just before I was repatriated, I overheard snippets of a discussion on the large patio at the resort. A diplomat and a lower level assistant were having a private conversation. The assistant asked the diplomat if he knew of the progress of a treasure transfer ordered by a Prince of the Imperial House."

"Prince Chichibu?"

"Hai. One and the same."

"What did this low level politico say?"

"I only heard small parts of the conversation, but I did hear the words gold and transfer, as well as the mention of caves, tunnels and underground complexes." He paused a moment. "And one other thing. The Philippines."

Finding A Way

"The Philippines?" Sakura roared. "No, absolutely not."

"But this could be the lead we are looking for," I protested. "The lead to the gold I saw stolen in Singapore."

Sakura stood from behind his desk and walked to me where I slouched down in a small office chair. He towered over me like a teacher who was about to verbally discipline his student. "I'm paying you to be a reporter, a war correspondent—*not* a treasure hunter."

He picked up several sheets of paper off his desk. "And speaking of reporting, *what the hell do you call this?*" He waved my interview with Hiyakawa under my nose. "A resort? Croquet? Nature walks along a lake? I'm supposed to print this? To say that it's a wonderful life for Japanese to live in America?"

He slammed the papers on his desk. "Not only will the censors kill the story, I would bet your life that I'd get a visit from the secret police accusing me of treason and utter incompetence."

Having been through his rants before, I sat quietly and waited for Sakura to calm down.

After a minute of muttering and cursing, he plopped back down on his chair and spoke slowly and deliberately. "Now. I want you to interview any other repatriates and find one that had a terrible *vacation* in America. And you better do it before our competition does." He stuck his cigar in his mouth. "Are we clear?"

Reprimanded, I slunk out of Sakura's office and out of the

building itself. Although I had been thoroughly scolded, it left me even more determined.

I'll find a way to get to the Philippines as a war correspondent, I told myself. *With or Without Sakura's help or permission.*

The Moral Tour

"Gomen'nasai," Yamamoto offered. "I'm sorry for the loss of your son."

"Hai," Fujiyama replied mournfully. "Domo."

Yamamoto stared out the window of the Mitsubishi *Betty* bomber, which took them to Rabaul to kickoff the first leg of the Admiral's morale tour through the South Pacific. In particular, he wanted to personally thank the troops that were still recovering from their ordeal on Guadalcanal.

Fujiyama observed the Admiral's pensive expression and noticed for the first time how much the man had aged over the last few years. During the Guadalcanal conflict his hair had turned snowy white. His words, too, reflected his fatigue. They demonstrated that he had become weary of war and even of life itself.

"Many young men have died in this war," Yamamoto said quietly. He sighed, turned his weary eyes on Fujiyama and spoke in a bare whisper. "So I believe the time has come for me to die, too."

Fujiyama was shocked by his Admiral's admission. He disagreed, and voiced his stance, telling Yamamoto that he was needed more than ever before.

Yamamoto smiled an empty smile and just patted Fujiyama on the shoulder. "There are many that do not hold your opinion. Many that would like to see me removed."

Both men were left to their own thoughts for a few moments. Fujiyama ventured to ask Yamamoto a question he had waiting to ask for some time. "Sir, I'd like my own command. I want to return to sea commanding my own ship."

Yamamoto's eyes drew kindly. "Hai. I suppose you have earned it. A fighter pilot should have his own command. I'll arrange it tomorrow. Before we leave on the 18th." As soon as Yamamoto voiced the date, the two men realized its significance.

"That's the one-year anniversary of the bombing of Tokyo," Fujiyama mused. "The Doolittle Raid."

"Hai. And the impetus for my plan to expand the Empire boundaries into the far Pacific." The Admiral's voice trailed off as if he had been unplugged.

Fujiyama surmised Yamamoto was thinking the same as he. *Those plans had been crushed at Coral Sea, Midway, and Guadalcanal.*

The Plot Sprung

"How long can we keep the new code books from South Pacific Command?" Prince Chichibu asked as he swirled warm sake in his cup. The Prince was extremely particular and insisted in stocking only the very best rice wine in his well-appointed office.

"A few days perhaps. A week at the most." Sato replied, running his fingers over the ceremonial Samurai sword facing him on Chichibu's regal desk.

Sato always envied that sword, a symbol of the Chrysanthemum Throne that had been handed down from Prince to Prince over the centuries.

"And if someone should question the reasons for the delay?"

"We'll simply say there were transit problems," Sato smirked, which caused his facial scar to project from his cheek even further. "With the Americans hampering our lines of communications more and more in the Pacific, the excuse will be acceptable for a short amount of time."

"And you really hope the Americans will act on the opportunity? Suppose they can't break the old code."

"We don't know that for a fact, but we've had our suspicions. That's why we frequently change the naval codes." He slid his neatly manicured finger off the sword. "Even if they don't, Yamamoto is exposing himself by flying all around the South Pacific command on his inspection tour."

He reclined back in his chair and sipped some sake. "Just in case,

I've taken certain precautions. We have instructed the naval base at Truk to radio ahead of Yamamoto's tour to expect him."

"Good," Chichibu replied. "Very good." And he waited for Sato to refill their sake cups.

Bushwacked

"We arrive on Balalae Island at 0800 hours," Ugaki said, reading off the itinerary of the inspection tour to Yamamoto. "You inspect the airfield there in the morning and leave for Bougainville promptly at 1200 hours."

"We'll take two planes," Fujiyama noted. "One for you, Sir, and the other with Ugaki and myself."

Yamamoto nodded his approval. "By the way, Fujiyama, I've arranged for you to command your own ship. A fleet carrier." He smiled warmly. "It's the best I could do in the current state of affairs."

Fujiyama laughed at Yamamoto's understatement. He was more than satisfied and thanked the Admiral several times.

The group headed for the airfield and promptly boarded two Betty bombers. As they soared away from Rabaul, escorted by nine Zero fighters, cheers erupted from the Japanese soldiers who lined both sides of the runway.

The first hour of the flight proved uneventful, but that quickly changed.

"Enemy fighters ahead," the pilot's voiced boomed over the intercom.

Yamamoto's bomber pilot immediately directed their attention upon a number of American Army P-38 Lightnings diving straight at the Bettys.

Both Bettys took decisive maneuvers, diving straight down to gain speed, leveling out just above the jungle canopy, while the

Zeros immediately engaged the enemy planes. One Zero was hit and spun into the jungle, exploding upon impact. The other escorting Japanese fighters desperately tried to prevent the American planes from reaching the unarmed bombers but to no avail.

A team of P-38s bore down upon Yamamoto's bomber; one of the fighters flew at right angles to Yamamoto's Betty, spewing tracer bullets at the metal hulk. The enemy fighter's cannon fire tore into the bomber's left engine and wing, leaving behind it shredded steel and a trail of black smoke.

The damaged Betty, spitting flame, suddenly lost its wing, causing it to spin out of control and crash into the jungle. A ball of fire erupted in a savage explosion, and only thick black smoke and unchecked flames remained of the bomber.

Fujiyama and Ugaki watched the scene of horror unfold before their eyes. They feared they too would share Yamamoto's fate.

And correctly so.

The P-38 fighters now turned their attention to Fujiyama's plane and descended upon the helpless bomber as it soared over the jungle and out towards sea. Bullets tore through the outer shell of the bomber, showering the interior of the plane with shards of metal, killing everyone but Fujiyama, Ugaki, and the pilot.

Cannon fire continued to be unleashed from the enemy fighter, tearing into the right wing of the Betty and it burst into flames. Ugaki and Fujiyama grabbed at their armrests and tucked their heads low as the pilot skimmed over the choppy surface of the water and crash-landed the Betty into the sea.

✷ ✷ ✷

"The Admiral?" Fujiyama mumbled. His voice was barely audible as he tried to sit up on his bed in the hospital ward on Rabaul. "What about the Admiral?"

"Please, you need to rest," coaxed a young nurse who was as wide as she was tall. She was dressed all in white and wore a small back and white cap adorned with the insignia of the Imperial Navy.

190

"You were hurt badly but you'll survive. You and Admiral Ugaki were extremely lucky," a navy doctor explained as he approached Fujiyama's bed. "You were the only survivors of the crash." He glanced through Fujiyama's medical chart. "Your right leg and hip are broken, and you have a dislocated shoulder. In a couple of months, perhaps longer, you'll be back on your feet."

"Ugaki?"

"Luckier than you," the nurse replied. "Suffered only a broken arm."

"But the Admiral?" Fujiyama pressed. "What about Yamamoto?"

The doctor shook his head. "He was found dead, still strapped in his seat, with two bullet wounds to the back of his head."

Once again, Fujiyama attempted to sit up, but it was too painful. "But how. How did the Americans know?"

The doctor just shook his head.

"Where are his remains?" Fujiyama solemnly asked.

"His staff cremated his remains at Buin," the doctor replied. "His ashes were returned to Tokyo aboard the battleship *Musashi*." He handed Fujiyama's medical record to the nurse. "It's a devastating blow to Japan, but we will have to move on without him." He patted Fujiyama on the arm. "I'm told you will have your own ship soon. Rest now and heal, then plan your revenge after that."

Tokyo

"I hope you will be comfortable here, Connor-san," Mai said as they entered the house in the residential Shirokane district of Tokyo.

Connor noticed that their home, unlike the Fujiyama's, was very common. The traditional Japanese house was smaller and built of wooden columns on top of a flat foundation made of packed earth and stones. The kitchen and hallways had wooden flooring, whereas the living room was covered with tatami. A sturdy wooden roof with deep eaves protected the house from the hot summer sun.

As in his home in Hiroshima, Connor took off his shoes and put on room slippers lying near the front door.

"You can stay in my brother's room while he is away at sea," Aiko added as they entered.

"Come," Mai said. "It's time for dinner. Perhaps you would like Aiko to show you a little bit of Tokyo tomorrow before she has to go to work.

"Hai," Aiko sweetly replied. "I would be happy to."

Yes. Connor thought. *I would like that. I would like that very much.*

Connor awoke the next morning well-rested and made his way to the kitchen for breakfast. When he arrived in the clean and organized room, he saw an arrangement of flowers on the dining table. But *arrangement* wasn't the accurate word for it since these displays were more like artistic compositions.

Connor asked Mai about them while she prepared breakfast.

"Aiko arranged them. They're called *Ikebana*—a Japanese cultural ideal or fine art that encompasses the best of aesthetics, spirituality, discipline, and harmony with nature. It's one of the Japanese arts a geisha has to learn."

Surprised, Connor said, "Aiko is a geisha?"

"Hai."

"I see you are admiring my Ikebana," Aiko boasted as she entered the kitchen.

Connor nodded his approval, still feeling somewhat shy around the young woman.

Just as they were finishing breakfast, the front door opened, and three young naval officers entered the kitchen.

"Daiki!" smiled Mei. "You're training cruise is over?"

But the young ensign's attention was focused on Connor. "Who is that?" he muttered, not caring that Connor could hear the disdain in his voice.

Mai kept her smile, but spoke emphatically. "This is Connor. He is a guest in our home and should be treated as such." She turned to Connor. "This is Daiki Onaga, my son."

Connor put out his hand. "Nice to meet you."

Daiki ignored Connor's outstretched hand. "Is he staying here?"

"Yes," Aiko retorted. "And as mother said, he is our *guest*."

Daiki shot Connor a malicious look. "He's no guest of mine, and if he stays here, I'm going somewhere else." He motioned to the other ensigns and then stomped out of the house.

Connor could see that Mai was embarrassed. She stared down at the floor, her face flushing red. "I'm so sorry for my son's behavior."

"The militarists have poisoned our young and dishonored our culture," Aiko remarked. She bowed her head as well. "They have corrupted what it means to be Japanese. Please accept our apologies."

She lightly touched Connor's hand, and he felt a warm tingle of pleasure arc through his body.

"Why don't you let me show you the Japan *I* know," Aiko said softly. "The true Japan."

A Tour

That afternoon, Aiko walked with Connor through parts of Tokyo showing him the finer aspects of Japanese culture, but Connor found himself more interested in the company.

As they walked, she pointed out a tall building on their right. "That's the Imperial Hotel, a famous Tokyo landmark. It was designed by an American, Frank Lloyd Wright, and, I am told, is undoubtedly one of the most unsuitably designed buildings in the world."

"How so?" asked Connor, intrigued by something American.

"It has abnormally low ceilings that make the rooms excessively hot in the summer, while the maze of useless passages become drafty and bitterly cold in the winter." She paused a moment before continuing. "But it *does* have one unique claim to fame. It was the only major building to survive the devastating 1923 earthquake."

As they entered the Ginza, Connor pointed to a Western-style building. "What is *that*?"

"That's the Kabuki-za, where they hold *kabuki* plays."

"Kabuki?"

"Loosely translated," she replied, "as *singing and dancing*. You might be interested to know that all the roles, even the female roles, are played by men."

"All men, huh?"

"Hai. But the plays have changed over the years," she said with a tinge of despair in her voice. "Before the war, the plays would be written to appeal to all types of audiences. The first part of the play would deal with some quiet domestic life in the country. This would be followed by some blood-and-thunder historical dramas, then a boisterous and erotic comedy. Then the evening would be rounded out with a Japanese ballet."

She stared at the Kabuki-za, and her tone sharpened. "Now the menu of the play has changed. It's all blood-and-thunder to reflect rabid patriotism and the virtue of dying for one's country. No other themes are allowed. The ordinary aims, aspirations, and love of human beings are excluded."

When they arrived at the Sumida River, small, pink flowers blossomed from the limbs of trees that lined the banks. The cherry blossom trees were in full riotous bloom.

"You are lucky Connor-san. This is the season for the blooming of the cherry blossoms. Are you familiar with this tree?"

Connor nodded. "Yes. The Fujiyama's have one at their house."

As they continued their city tour, they passed large groups of families and friends gathered around and under the vivid crimson trees enjoying a festival of food, drink, and music.

"A total of one hundred cherry blossom trees were planted according to the order of Tokugawa Yoshimune, our eighth shogun, in the year 1717. Since then, many people have planted trees in this area." She waved her hands in front of her. "The importance of the cherry blossom tree in Japanese culture, Connor-san, goes back hundreds of years. They represent the fragility and the beauty of life."

Her voice took on melodic tone. And her words appeared to dance from her lips. "It's a reminder that life is almost overwhelmingly beautiful, but that it is also tragically short."

Connor could agree with that. What was it he heard about life once? Nasty, brutish, and short? He could agree with that. But the presence of this enticing woman softened that belief.

She gazed at the blossom trees and reflected, "When we Japanese ponder the cherry blossoms, they remind us of how precious life is, and how it should not be discarded willfully."

Connor thought back on Yoshi and Hiryo's enthusiasm for having the honor of dying for the Emperor, and sensed Aiko saw the waste in that very belief.

"As we marvel at their beauty, we aren't just thinking about the flowers themselves, but also about the larger meaning and deep cultural traditions the cherry blossom tree represents."

Aiko noticed that Connor seemed distracted and also sensed a feeling of antagonism in his temperament. Or perhaps it was pain. She felt it the first day at the hospital. *Was it towards her? Or perhaps Japan?* But being polite, she did not try to pry.

They finished their walk along the banks of the river and caught a cab to downtown. "There is an exciting festival going on this month that should be fun for us this afternoon. It's called the *Sanja Matsuri.*"

Thirty minutes later, the cab dropped them off to the sounds of flutes, whistles, chanting, and taiko drums flooding the street. It was a parade, but unlike any parade Connor had ever seen before. A procession of massive sacred altars called *mikoshi* were carried and shaken vehemently by a half-dozen men each. Each man held a pole supporting the mikoshi, all of them shouting and directing the others to avoid the one-ton mikoshi from colliding with the street shops.

"Why do they jerk them up and down like that?" Connor noted. "They'll drop those floats on top of them."

"It's to intensify the power of the *Kami*," Aiko explained. "To bestow good luck upon the neighborhood."

As the procession passed, Aiko noticed Connor's expression turn to dismay. "*Yakuza,*" he said under his breath.

Passing before them was a mikoshi manned by several fully tattooed Yakuza. All of them were wearing tight, white fundoshi, a traditional Japanese loincloth.

"You know of the Yakuza?" questioned Aiko.

"I've... heard of them," he replied.

Aiko accepted his explanation. "This is the only time of year are they are allowed to show the totality of their tattooed bodies in public." She smiled at Connor. "It's a very colorful display, no?"

Connor shrugged and changed the subject. "Are you hungry? I am."

She nodded. "Wait here and enjoy the parade. I'll get us something to eat." She arched her eyebrows. "Something traditional."

"Nothing *too* traditional, please."

Aiko laughed. "Of course. Be right back."

Connor continued to watch the parade of colorful floats when a strong hand grabbed the back of his shoulder and spun him around.

"*Ijin!*" spit Daiki. The two other young officers that were with him at Aiko's home were with him as well.

"I don't want any trouble," Connor replied. But his entire body tensed, ready for a fight. He saw the chances of that mounting as the three young men quickly surrounded him.

The scene was ready to explode when a voice ordered, "Stop it, Daiki!" Aiko approached them with her hands full of rice cakes.

Her brother looked at Aiko and sneered, "He is our enemy. He is nothing but a coward."

"*Mind me!*" Aiko demanded.

"I don't have to obey you," Daiki snapped. Then under his breathe, "Hinin."

"Maybe not me," Aiko threatened. "But you will Matsumuro."

At the sound of the name, the three men immediately backed off. Daiki grunted and the trio melted into the crowd around them.

Connor wondered, *What power does Matsumuro have over those three young officers?*

Whoever he was, Connor was glad Aiko knew him.

Geisha

It was late afternoon by the time they returned to Aiko's home. Mai was preparing dinner and inquired about their day.

"Connor learned a little more of what it used to be like to be Japanese," Aiko smiled. "But I must get ready for work soon."

After dinner, Connor was drinking tea and giving Mai an account of his life in America when he heard tight little clacking sounds enter the room. He turned to see Aiko dressed in full-fledged geisha attire, and he nearly dropped his teacup.

Her face had transformed into stark white make-up, and her eyebrows were concealed and re-drawn. Pink eye shadow had been applied to the corners of her eyes and jet-black eyeliner finished out the look. A clean line of red lipstick stood out from the very center of her lower lip. She wore a wide, white bow on the kimono's long sleeves, which were colorful and intricately adorned with embroidery and hand-painted designs. High wooden shoes, to keep her kimono from dragging on the ground, completed the makeover.

Aiko bowed to Connor and her mother, and with small precise steps, she left the house without speaking.

Mai watched Connor's eyes follow Aiko out of the house. There was a puzzled expression on his face. "Is there something wrong, Connor-san?"

Connor didn't quite know how to phrase his words so he just blurted it out. "We ran into Daiki and his friends today."

"Oh?"

"He called Aiko a *hinin*."

"I see," she said and picked up a cup of tea from the table. "Being a true geisha is an honor. When girls become full-fledged geisha's they are called *geiko*. If a girl begins her training to be a geisha before she is twenty, she is called a *maiko*, meaning *child dancer*. A girl or young woman can become a geisha even if she wasn't a maiko, but if she had been a maiko, she would enjoy much more prestige. Aiko was such a child."

Connor waited as Mai searched for the best words to continue.

"Aiko attends parties and tea houses where she entertains and acts as hostess. She pours tea, sings and dances, plays instruments, and chats with the guests. Sort of the *life of the party* as Americans say."

She sipped some of her tea. "If you translate geisha into English, you get *artist*."

"But is she... a hinin—a prostitute?"

Mai raised an eyebrow. "Because the geisha is much coveted, prostitutes have called themselves geishas to bring in more customers, but you will notice a distinct difference, and that is their attire."

"How?" Connor asked. He was not so much interested in the cultural lecture, but to determine if Aiko really was a prostitute.

Mai took another sip of her tea. "Both girls wear a kimono. And over their kimono is an *obi*, a sash. Geisha's tie their obi in the back, and prostitutes tie it in the front."

"Why?"

Mai smiled. "You can't tie it yourself if it's in the back, and if you're a prostitute, you're going to need to tie it and untie it throughout the day."

"Makes sense," Connor replied. "But does she get paid as a geisha?"

"Some girls, like Aiko, have a *danna*, a patron. The danna pays for all of their expenses, sort of like a mistress, but different. So, now you see?"

Connor nodded slowly and stared into his green tea.

Mai noticed Connor's brooding grow darker. "Are you not happy here, Connor-san?"

Connor snapped out of his introspection. "I'm quite happy here. With you and Aiko. But..."

Mai held Connor's hand. "Please. Tell me."

Her touch and empathetic eyes reminded him so much of his adopted mother. "This place... this city... this time... is no different from where I was before. I was an ijin then, and I'm still an ijin now. I don't know where I belong."

Mai patted his hand. "Hai. You will find your way, Connor-san. You are different. You are special, and you will find your way through your Nurikabe someday."

Connor ears perked up. *Nurikabe.* That's exactly the word Miyoko had used.

"Domo, mama-san," Connor replied. "Domo arigato."

Truly Grave

As 1943 progressed; Connor enjoyed the company of Aiko in Tokyo, Hiyakawa mourned the death of his wife while serving these troubled days of Japan as Assistant to the Lord Keeper of the Privy Seal, Fujiyama recovered in a Rabaul naval hospital, and I was stuck interviewing the repatriated Japanese from American interment with occasional stories of the worsening effects of war rationing on the nation.

One night at his home for dinner, Hiyakawa informed me of an incident during a war meeting in the Palace. Field Marshall Hajime Sugiyama told Hirohito that the American advance through the Solomon Islands could not be stopped.

The Emperor, who over the months had become increasingly worried and impatient with the progress of war, was quiet as he usually was when presented with bad news. Then he gazed to his High Command and spoke bluntly. "When and where are you *ever* going to put up a good fight? And when are you ever going to fight a decisive battle?" His cold stare turned directly on Sugiyama. "And it is to you that I order that we work with the Navy to implement better military preparation and give adequate supply to our soldiers fighting in Rabaul. Have my orders been unclear?"

"So troubling was the situation," Hiyakawa confided, "that the Emperor actually announced that Japan's situation was now, *truly grave.*"

I thanked Hiyakawa for sharing this bit of news, but didn't tell him that Sakura would not print any of it and, like so many of my reports deemed critical of the war effort or defeatist, my stories would sit unused, awaiting the day I could account for them.

But there was one respite from my tedious news assignments—Yamamoto. I covered his State Funeral, which was a first for a naval officer since all other State Funerals were reserved for Imperial Princes. Yamamoto was awarded the title of Marshall and the Order of the Chrysanthemum. His ashes were put to rest in the public Tama Cemetery in Tokyo.

After covering that moving ceremony, I expressed my continued dissatisfaction with my other assignments to Sakura and was quite surprised and disappointed when he offered me the opportunity to cover the Axis news in Europe. I quickly declined. I'd rather tolerate the malevolence of the Japanese military than the madness of Nazi Germany.

The only one of us that had anywhere near a congenial respite from the brutal effects of this ill-planned war was Connor, for he was enjoying the intimate company of Aiko.

Pikunikku

One afternoon in July, as Connor prepared to set out for a short foray into Tokyo, he spotted Aiko sitting crosslegged at the small dinning room table. She was writing something in smooth brush strokes on a sheet of white rice paper.

"That's beautiful," he said as he gazed over her long, streaming black hair that swept over her shoulder. "What is it?"

She looked up at him and smiled a smile that always gave him a flush of warm feelings. These emotions were nothing like what he felt for Kodo—or his adopted sister Suki who, he had a deeper feeling of caring, of respect, of admiration.

Whatever the case, he was slowly being enchanted by Aiko's gentle beauty and charm.

"It's called *Shodo*," she replied as she applied a gentle stroke of ink to the canvas. "It's an art requiring many years of practice and considered essential learning, especially for geishas, for an accomplished person in Japanese society."

"I've never seen that kind of writing before. I mean... it's so beautiful."

Her voice took on a slight air of bitterness. "All we see today in public is the crude militaristic posters written in crude script that matches their crude idea of what Japan is suppose to be."

Beautiful and sensitive, but with strong sentiments, Connor thought.

She appeared to shake off the resentment when she stared at

Connor's earnest face. "I have the day to myself," she said. "I want to take you on a pikunikku. I think in English it's called a picnic."

✷ ✷ ✷

It was a sunny, warm day in September as Aiko toted a picnic basket and led Connor to the Tokyo train station. After a short cab ride, they boarded the train and headed out of the city.

"We need to leave the city to have a picnic? Where are we going?" Connor asked.

Aiko simply pointed out the window. "There."

Connor gazed out the panel of glass toward a massive mountain range that loomed in the distance. "Mt. Fuji?"

"Hai. We'll picnic on its slopes."

They made small talk as the train traveled through the country-side of little villages, rice paddies, and small farms, with Connor learning more of the geisha and Japanese cultural traditions. Little could he know that he would personally learn of two traditions that day—one formal and elegant, and the other, though formal, rather unnerving.

A couple of hours later, they finally arrived at their destination. After disembarking the train, they made their way to Lake Kawa-guchiko, one of the five lakes at the northern base of Mt. Fuji.

"This is one of the best places in Japan to view Mt. Fuji," Aiko stated.

Connor had to agree. The view of the dormant, snow peaked volcano of Mt. Fuji reflected against the mirror-like waters of Lake Kawaguchiko was an incredible sight to behold.

They walked around the lake as Aiko's calm gentle voice echoed the feelings that Connor held inside.

"There," she pointed. "That's the Fujisan Hongu Sengen Taisha Shrine. Those who climb Mt. Fuji stop there and pray for a safe journey."

But even with the sheer beauty all around him, Connor was more captivated by Aiko than the subject matter. Although Connor's stomach churned with fondness for this young woman, the surrounding environment felt magical.

The mountain views and clean, fresh air had a soothing affect on him. It almost made him forget the last few years—his alienation from a people he wanted so much to be a part of and the dishonor and dishonesty of Fujiyama.

Aiko noticed Connor's deep troubles, yet kept her thoughts to herself.

They arrived at a picturesque spot on the lake that offered an impressive view of the mountain, and Aiko began unpacking the basket and arranging their lunch on a grass mat.

"Why don't we have the picnic over there in the forest?" Connor asked. "It's much cooler than staying out here in the open."

Aiko shook her head. "That's the Aokigahara forest. The mysterious sea of trees."

"Huh?" Connor replied, cocking his head.

"It's not a very pleasant place. It's dense and harsh, filled with rocky, icy caverns shutting out everything but the natural sounds of the forest itself. Even at high noon, barely any sunlight can break through the trees." She looked at the trailhead leading into the forest. "Many believe the forest is filled with demons."

Connor eyed the wooden sign at the beginning of the trailhead. "What does it say?"

Without even looking, she said, "It urges suicidal visitors to think of their families and contact help."

"Suicides?"

"Hai. It's a popular place to die. People go there to end their lives." She laid out sweet rice cakes and pieces of cold chicken on the blanket as she spoke.

Connor dove right in, then noticed that Aiko was not touching the food. "What about you? Aren't you eating?"

"You are my guest, and what I do now is for you," she replied softly.

Connor's curiosity was peaking with every passing moment

he spent with this young woman. Once Aiko was satisfied that Connor had his fill, she withdrew from the basket a tea bowl, tea scoop, tea whisk, and a small packet of green powder. She then began to clean the tea serving utensils with a ritual of care and graceful movements.

Connor watched the ritual with intent interest as she added three scoops of the green powder to the tea bowl, whisked it into a thin paste, then added more water as needed to create a soup-like tea.

"The green paste is call *matcha* and this tea ceremony is called *Chanoyu*. It's for you. My guest. The *Shokyaku*."

She finished making the tea and added, "The ceremony is not just about drinking tea. It's about preparing a bowl of tea from my heart." She gave Connor an affectionate smile that made him blush.

Is she saying she loves me?

"Now," she said, "observe, and do as I do." She presented the prepared tea bowl in a ritual manner to Connor and bowed.

Connor realized he had to return the bow and did so.

"Now, rotate the bowl and take a drink. Then wipe the rim of the bowl."

Connor followed her instructions as closely as he could manage.

Aiko took the bowl from Connor and cleaned it thoroughly.

"If we had another Shokyaku present, they would repeat what you have just done." As she gathered up the bowl and utensils and returned them to the bamboo basket, Aiko nodded to Connor. "We must return to the city now."

"Going home?"

"No. Not quite yet," she smiled.

Another Old Tradition

They arrived back in Tokyo just as the sun was setting, and Aiko led Connor down a narrow street in a commercial district of the city.

"Where exactly are we going?" Connor asked.

"To show you another old tradition of Japan," she grinned.

They stopped at a small, two-story building with colorful streamers and banners hanging from the eaves. Like most of the buildings in the residential and commercial district in Tokyo, this structure was constructed of wood. The sound of someone plucking a stringed instrument and gentle singing voices emanated from inside the building.

They entered without knocking or announcing their arrival, Aiko led Connor to a tiny room near the front entrance. "Wait here," she instructed, then left him alone in the room.

Connor surveyed the room and quickly realized he was in some kind of bathroom. There was a small porcelain tub in the corner of the room with a showerhead installed on the wall. He waited patiently for Aiko's return and was surprised at who came through the door next.

Two young women dressed in light kimonos entered and approached Connor smiling and giggling. Connor stood, but before he could utter a single word, the two girls proceeded to undress him.

Connor had no idea what to do. Was this Aiko's idea? Should he allow the girls to undress him?

As confused thoughts rushed through his mind, the women

quietly finished undressing the teen and led Connor to the shallow tub. The girls proceeded to spray his body down and wash him with sweet-smelling soap, followed by a warm rinse.

When finished with their task, the girls bowed their way out of the room, giggling as they went and taking Connor's clothes with them.

Connor was left standing there, semi-dry, and completely naked.

A few moments later, Aiko entered the room. She wore only a white cotton towel, half-covered by her long, shimmering black hair. She smiled at seeing Connor's naked embarrassment and handed him a red silk kimono.

Holding out her hand she said softly, "Come."

Connor followed Aiko up the stairs to a room dimly lit by candles that cast flickering shadows against the wall. Flowers were arranged around a large bathtub and a flask of sake sat on a low table next to it. "Please, sit there," she said, pointing to a wooden stool by the door.

Connor complied, sitting and watching as Aiko filled the bathtub with hot water, then added a few drops of rose geranium and eucalyptus oils that cast a floral aroma throughout the room.

Satisfied that the tub had been filled to the desired level, she pulled her hair into a Samurai knot and invited him to the fragrant water.

Connor stood motionless as Aiko relieved him of his kimono, letting it slide effortlessly onto the floor. The silky feeling flowing against his freshly scrubbed skin was both sensual and erotic.

She took his hand and led him into the warm scented water, then deliberately and sensuously removed her cotton towel and stood in front of Connor in full nakedness.

She was breathtakingly exquisite. Every part of her. Aiko's skin was pale white, almost alabaster in the candlelight, and without a single visible blemish. The curves of her hips and breasts were flawless. Her stomach and thighs were both firm and supple.

Without a word, she climbed into the tub behind Connor,

kneeling behind him. Her arms embraced his shoulders and her soft breasts pressed against his back.

She began washing him with small handfuls of water. Up his arms, around his neck, down his chest, around his abdomen, gently over his genitalia, then proceeded to the legs and finishing with the feet. All her washing was conducted with slow deliberation and attentiveness to Connor's every pleasure.

Connor found himself fully aroused and wanted to say something, but Aiko put a soft fingertip against his lips. She plucked a Kyoho, a dark purple Japanese grape, from a bowl that lay next to the tub and placed it into his mouth.

This went on for several minutes when Aiko asked Connor to exit the tub. When he did, she handed him a soft white robe to put on. She gave him a warm smile and whispered, "Follow me."

Minutes later, Connor found himself in a bedroom, again lit by candles, and this time with the added scent of sweet incense. Aiko led him to the bed, laid him down and kissed his forehead.

But that was not enough for Connor. He reached up, gently pulled her towards him and gave her a passionate kiss.

Aiko responded in turn and the two wrapped themselves into a lover's embrace that led from the sensual to the erotic, and finally to a place that Connor had never experienced before.

Ownership

Aiko lay inside Connor's arms as he stroked her bare shoulders with the back of his fingers. Over the weeks that followed their initial love making, they had shared their bodies countless times, but despite that, Connor's mood swings seemed to be getting worse.

Aiko could sense he was troubled. "Connor-san, do I not please you anymore?"

He sat up abruptly and blurted out his worries. "I've lied to you," he said. He took her face between his hands and stared into her eyes. "And I hate lies. My life is filled with lies. In Japan. In America. Everywhere I go."

"What kind of lies?"

"I'm not American... at least not a full American. I am half-Japanese."

Aiko stood up, and her face broke out into a broad smile. "That is *good*. Why didn't you tell me before? You belong here. With me."

"I don't feel like I belong. Being half-Japanese or not, I still feel like an outsider." Connor proceeded to tell Aiko of his mother and father, his nanny, and his present anger and resentment toward Fujiyama.

"I understand, Connor. I do. But are you angry at being Japanese?"

"I'm angry at being *lied to*," he snapped. "Lied to by my mother. Lied to by my nanny." His jaws tightened. "And maybe worst of all, being lied to by Fujiyama."

Aiko caressed his hand. "Fujiyama loves you. You must know

that. He adopted you." She squeezed his hand in hers. "Is that why you came to stay with us? Because of your anger with Fujiyama?"

Connor nodded his head. "Fujiyama speaks of honor and loyalty. He speaks of the Samurai code. Yet he has no honor. He lied to me about my past."

Aiko turned and gazed out the window of her bedroom, searching for the right words. "Connor-san. You may have the wrong idea of the Samurai code."

"I don't understand what you mean. You either live by the code, or you don't."

"Over the last few months, I've tried to show you a different version of Japan that you were not exposed to before. Not only a *different* Japan but a *true* Japan—one not corrupted by the militarists and nationalists."

"But what about the Samurai code? Is there something that I don't understand?"

Aiko was quiet a moment before replying. "I know someone who can answer that question. Perhaps you would like to meet him."

He turned her towards him and gently held Aiko's face in his hands. "I know what I want. I want *you*, Aiko. I want you forever."

Aiko dropped her eyes and whispered. "That can never be.
"Why?"

"Because, Connor-san, I belong to someone else."

"Someone else?"

"I have a sponsor and he—"

"Hai. I know," Connor interjected. "Your mother told me. Does that mean you love him?"

"No. It's not like that," she replied. "But he owns me. It's the way it is."

"*Owns* you?"

Aiko nodded and was about to explain when Connor stood and blurted out, "Can I buy you from him?"

Aiko laughed a bitter, hallow laugh. "I am very expensive, Connor-san. Very." She slid her hand over his cheek. "But we can still see each other." She reached over, gave him a passionate kiss, and at first Connor resisted, but soon desire took over, and he found himself back on Aiko's bed.

Targeting Fujiyama

Colonel Sato and Major Takahashi were seated in one of the *buntais*, a Kempeitai field office outside of Tokyo, when Takahashi muttered in disgust. "Fujiyama survived. And with that, do you think he will take up Yamamoto's fervent cause in the Navy?"

"Possibly. He's currently recuperating in a naval hospital," Sato replied. "He may still pose a problem. If not him, there are many naval officers who hold defeatist views like Yamamoto. All they need is a leader. But we should take no chances with Fujiyama."

Sato raised his hand, knowing what his headstrong comrade was going to propose. "He cannot, must not, be touched in the hospital. Whether the Navy knows it or not, they are protecting him. We'll have to wait for a more discreet opportunity to handle the situation."

"The man is a cat," Takahashi mulled. "Many lives."

"Perhaps. But although we may not be able to eliminate him, we can intimidate him through his family." Sato's scarred face transformed into a hideous grin. "And this must be done *without* fingerprints to trace any action back to us."

A Message
From the Author

I relished writing this book! If you enjoyed the continuing story of the Fujiyama family and events involved with the growing conflict between the United States of America and the Empire of Japan during the Second World War, would you consider doing two things?

First, sign up for my newsletter at www.frankfiore.com, and I'll be sure you're the first to get news on the final installment in the Ijin Series, in addition to info about my other titles.

Second—and this is a big request—if you liked this story, would you consider leaving a review wherever you bought this book, or on your favorite social media platform? I want as many readers as possible to discover this story, and your voice can help do that. Leave a review and tell a friend! Word-of-mouth is still the best way to introduce this story to other readers.

Lastly, *Thank you!*

Thank you, dear reader, for giving your time to read this book. It means a lot that you trusted me as the author to entertain, and hopefully excite, you with this story. Stories need an audience, and I appreciate you being my audience for just a little while. Thank you.

I know, I know, there are plenty of historical details surrounding World War 2 that are common knowledge, but there are still lots of questions about the lives of our main characters that need answers. Like…

What happened to Kenta Hiyakawa?
Will Connor officially join the Japanese military?
Will Aiko win her freedom from her sponsor?
Will Fujiyama survive the assassination attempts by Sato and Takahashi?
And so, dear readers, just for you, here's—

Warrior Monk

"Where exactly are we?," Connor asked Aiko after the long train ride to the Namba Nankai station in Osaka, south of Tokyo. From there, they rode the express train on the Mount Koya Rail Line, then took the Mount Koya cable car to the top of the mountain.

"Mount Koya. Near the Shojoshin-in temple," she replied. "A very holy place and the home of Buddhist monks that dates back over a thousand years."

White clouds appeared below them as the cable car rumbled up the face of the mountain. Connor stared into the valley below and watched as the clouds began their habitual, silent advance up the slopes as if racing after them.

Upon arriving at the summit, he found himself standing on a mountaintop swathed in a cool breeze and surrounded by towering trees covered in a misty haze. Before them stood one of several ornate Japanese shrines.

At the end of a long, stone path, a cedar forest lined with elaborate lanterns beckoned them to enter. They stepped into the Shojoshin-in temple and were greeted by a diminutive, bald, Buddhist monk. "May I help you?" he asked respectfully.

Aiko bowed. "We're here to see Admiral Nakamura."

Connor was surprised at the request. "We're here to see an admiral?"

"A warrior monk."

"A warrior monk?" Connor questioned, confused.

Aiko placed her fingers to his lips to quiet him as the monk stretched out an arm from his black and white *kesa* robe as a sign to follow him. Connor and Aiko trailed after the man, walking through wooded aisles of a small residential area the temple. The architecture was both exquisite and ancient, making Connor feel as if he was entering a very precious place.

"Please wait here," the little monk instructed, pointing to a sitting area in a small garden of carefully arranged rocks, water falls, moss, pruned trees, and bushes. All around them, the gravel had been raked to represent ripples in water.

"It's a Zen garden," Aiko whispered. "It is intended to imitate the intimate essence of nature and to serve as an aid to meditation about the true meaning of life."

As they both sat enjoying the silence of the garden, they heard footsteps come up from behind them. They turned to see a tall, elderly Nipponese man approach. Connor guessed he must be eighty years old—perhaps older. Yet, there was an inner and outer strength to him that defied his age. He walked in an odd combination of military and contemplative style and appeared both intimidating and accessible at the same time.

Aiko stood and bowed deeply. "Nakamura-san. I would like to introduce you to my dear friend, Connor Fujiyama."

As Connor rose and bowed to Nakamura, he gave the boy a probing look. "Fujiyama? An American with a Japanese last name."

Aiko proceed to explain how Connor was adopted by the Fujiyamas.

"Did you say Akihito Fujiyama?"

Aiko nodded.

Nakamura finally turned his attention to Connor. "You must be very proud. Akihito Fujiyama served under my command in the Great War. He was not only an outstanding fighter pilot in my Navy, but a man with great honor."

Connor didn't respond, and Nakamura sensed much tension and conflict in the boy.

Major Historical Characters
Mentioned In The Book

Emperor Hirohito—Emperor of Japan. A peaceful man. However, he is no politician.

Vice-Admiral Yamamoto—a leading advocate of peace and reason in the Imperial Navy. He was the mastermind behind the attack on Pearl Harbor.

Prince Chichibu—Emperor Hirohito's brother, has repeatedly counseled the Emperor to implement direct imperial rule, even if that means suspending the constitution and creating a military dictatorship.

General Minoru Genda—A Imperial Japanese Navy flight officer, JASDF general and politician. Genda is best known for helping to plan the attack on Pearl Harbor. He was also the third Chief of Staff of the Japan Air Self-Defense Force.

Mitsuo Fuchida—A captain in the Imperial Japanese Navy Air Service and a bomber observer in the Imperial Japanese Navy before and during World War II. Best known for leading the first wave of air attacks on Pearl Harbor, Fuchida was responsible for the coordination of the entire aerial attack.

Field Marshall Hajime Sugiyama—Army Minister in 1937, Sugiyama was a driving force behind the launch of hostilities against China in retaliation for the Marco Polo Bridge Incident. After being named the Army's Chief of Staff in 1940, he became a leading advocate for expansion into Southeast Asia and preventive war against the United States.

General Tomoyuki Yamashita—A general in the Imperial Japanese Army,. Yamashita led Japanese forces during the invasion of Malaya and Battle of Singapore. His accomplishment of conquering Malaya and Singapore in 70 days earned him the sobriquet *The Tiger of Malaya*. Convicted of war crimes after the war and executed in 1946.

Chūichi Nagumo—was an admiral in the Imperial Japanese Navy during World War II. Nagumo led Japan's main carrier battle group, the Kido Butai, in the attack on Pearl Harbor, the Indian Ocean raid and the Battle of Midway.

Major Fictional Characters
Mentioned In The Book

Yoshihara Koga—a Japanese-American reporter is introduced to tell Connor's story.

Connor Williams—an American teenager is an innocent soul coming of age against the backdrop of an ill-conceived war. Soon to lead a flight of kamikaze planes against the U.S. Fleet of Okinawa.

Akihito Fujiyama—a Commander and fighter pilot in the Imperial Japanese Navy. Fujiyama acts as military attaché to the U.S. Navy. He lives with his wife, Miyoko, and their sons. Hiryo is fourteen and Yoshi is thirteen.

Kenta Hiyakawa—works with the Japanese Foreign Office. He is a thorn in the side of the militarists. He is a distant cousin of the emperor, thus a confirmation of the rumors that he has the emperor's ear.

Barbara Hiyakawa—wife of Hiyakawa, a tall, elegant Caucasian American woman with short auburn hair. She is bold and outspoken.

Meiko Nemoto—Connor's Japanese nanny, who cares for him alone after his mother dies and his father abandons him.

Miyoko Fujiyama—a gentle and loving woman, wife to Fujiyama.

Tomoko Sakura—Yoshihara's editor, who sees himself as an ethical Samurai for truth, like his hero, Edward G. Robinson.

Haru Sato—a Kempeitai colonel on the Supreme Military Council that sits in Army/Navy Imperial Headquarters. Part of the military's police arm and leader of the Yakuza.

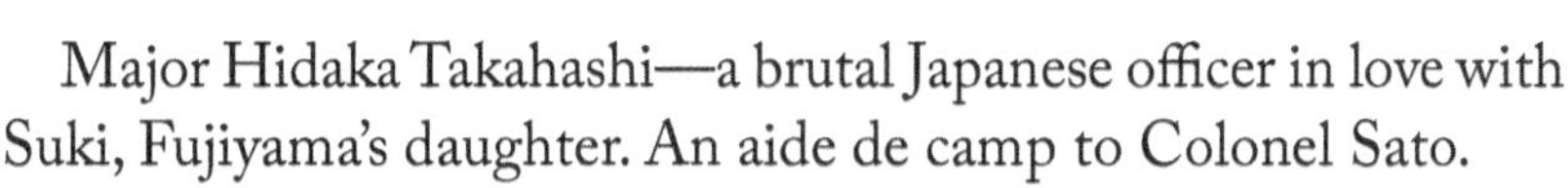

Major Hidaka Takahashi—a brutal Japanese officer in love with Suki, Fujiyama's daughter. An aide de camp to Colonel Sato.

Kenji—youngest Fujiyama son enamored with American culture.

Suki—Fujiyama's only daughter, a young girl, just shy of 5 feet, with long, black hair that hangs over dark eyes that dance on high cheekbones. Connor is enamored with her.

Mai—Miyoko's sister. She offers to host Connor after his release from prision.

Kodo Tento—Goro Yoshida and Jiro Miyagi—members of the Yakuza. Connor is attracted to Kodo, the tattooed girl. This group is led by Sato who is also part of the Kempeitei.

Taka—a fellow soldier who dreams of glory, yet ends up abandoning Yoshi and being a source of conflict.

Sgt. Gunso—a platoon leader. Gunso is quite large for a Japanese, big and as intimidating as any sergeant could ever be. Rumor around the platoon is that he came from a family of sumo wrestlers.

Genero Nakatomi—a reporter, from one of the Japanese news services.

Mrs. Ito—an old lady who owned the tobacco store down the street from the Fujiyama's and who headed the local neighborhood association.

Black Patch—close school friend of Kenji's. He is called Black Patch because of the dark brown birthmark that covers almost a quarter of his face.

Niko Kimura—aka Little Glass Eye, a stout, disheveled looking man, and after losing his left eye in China, Niko was relieved of service. Now he is a paid civilian guard at the prison.

Williams—Connor's cruel American father.

Aiko—niece to Miyako, daughter of Mai. She is a geisha. Connor falls in love with her.

Daiki Onaga—Mai's son. He is an ensign in the Japanese Navy.

Nakamura—a warrior monk with an unusual Samurai past.

Matsumuro—the wealthy *sponsor* of Aiko.

About the Author

Frank F. Fiore is a five-star rated author of novels in multiple genres including Contemporary Fiction, Tecno-Thrillers, Action/Adventures, Sci-Fi, Historical Fiction, and Westerns. He lives in Arizona with his fetching wife, Lynne.

Connect with Frank online at:

www.frankfiore.com

Also Available From

WordCrafts Press

In Times Like These
Gail Kittleson

Angela's Treasures
Marian Rizzo

The Pruning
Jan Cline

The Restless Earth
Alan Cockrell

Oh, to Grace
Abby Rosser

www.wordcrafts.net